As We Forgive Them

As We
Forgive Them
William Le Queux

MINT EDITIONS

As We Forgive Them was first published in 1904.

This edition published by Mint Editions 2021.

ISBN 9781513280905 | E-ISBN 9781513285924

Published by Mint Editions®

 **MINT
EDITIONS**

minteditionbooks.com

Publishing Director: Jennifer Newens
Design & Production: Rachel Lopez Metzger
Project Manager: Micaela Clark
Typesetting: Westchester Publishing Services

Contents

I

The Stranger in Manchester

"Dead! And he's carried his secret with him to his grave!"

"Never!"

"But he has. Look! His jaw has dropped. Can't you see the change, man!"

"Then he's carried out his threat after all!"

"By Heaven, he has! We've been fools, Reggie—utter idiots!" I whispered.

"So it seems. I confess that I fully expected he'd tell us the truth when he knew that the end had really come."

"Ah! you didn't know him as I did," I remarked bitterly. "He had a will of iron and a nerve of steel."

"Combined with the constitution of a horse, or he'd been dead long ago. But we've been outwitted—cleanly outwitted by a dying man. He defied us, laughed at our ignorance to the very last."

"Blair was no fool. He knew what knowledge of the truth meant to us—a huge fortune. So he simply kept his secret."

"And left us in penniless chagrin. Well, although we've lost thousands, Gilbert, I can't help admiring his dogged determination. He went through a lot, recollect, and he's been a good friend to us—very good—so I suppose we really oughtn't to abuse him, however much we regret that he didn't let us into his secret."

"Ah, if only those white lips could speak! One word, and we'd both be rich men," I said in regret, gazing upon the dead, white face, with its closed eyes and closely clipped beard, lying there upon the pillow.

"He intended to hold his secret from the very first," remarked my tall friend, Reginald Seton, folding his arms as he stood on the opposite side of the bed. "It isn't given to every man to make such a discovery as he made. It took him years to solve the problem, whatever it was; but that he really succeeded in doing so we can't for a moment doubt."

"And his profit was over a million sterling," I remarked.

"More like two, at the very lowest estimate. Recollect how, when we first knew him, he was in dire want of a sovereign—and now? Why, only last week he gave twenty thousand to the Hospital Fund. And all as the result of solving the enigma which for so long we have tried to discover in vain. No, Gilbert, he hasn't played the square game by us. We assisted him, put him on his legs, and all that, and instead of revealing to us the key to the secret which he discovered, and which placed him among the wealthiest men of London, he point-blank refused, even though he knew that he must die. We lent him money in the old days, financed him, kept Mab at school when he had no funds, and—"

"And he repaid us every penny—with interest," I interposed. "Come; don't let's discuss him here. The secret is lost for ever, that's enough." And I drew the sheet over the poor dead face—the countenance of Burton Blair, the man who, during the past five years, had been one of London's mysteries.

A strange, adventurous life, a career more remarkable, perhaps, than half those imagined by writers of romance, had been brought abruptly to an end, while the secret of the source of his enormous wealth—the secret which we both had for the past five years longed to share, because we were in a sense justly entitled to participate in its advantages—had gone with him to that bourne whence none return.

The apartment in which we stood was a small, rather well-furnished bedroom in the *Queen's Hotel*, Manchester. The window looked out upon the dark facade of the Infirmary, while to that chamber of the dead there came the roar and bustle of the traffic and trams in Piccadilly. His story was assuredly one of the strangest that any man has ever told. Its mystery, as will be seen, was absolutely bewildering.

The light of the cheerless February afternoon was quickly fading, and as we turned softly to descend and inform the hotel manager of the fatal termination of the seizure, I noticed that the dead man's suit-case stood in the corner, and that his keys were still in it.

"We had better take possession of these," I remarked, locking the bag and transferring the small bunch to my pocket. "His executors will want them."

Then we closed the door behind us, and going to the office imparted the unwelcome intelligence that a death had occurred in the hotel. The manager was, however, quite prepared to learn such news, for, half an hour before, the doctor had declared that the stranger could not live. His case had been hopeless from the very first.

Briefly, the facts were as follows. Burton Blair had bidden his daughter Mabel farewell, left his house in Grosvenor Square on the previous morning, and had taken the ten-thirty express from Euston to

Manchester, where he had said he had some private business to transact. Just before the train arrived at Crewe, he suddenly became unwell, and was discovered by one of the luncheon-car attendants in a state of collapse in one of the first-class compartments. Brandy and restoratives being administered, he revived sufficiently to travel on to Manchester, being assisted out of the train at London Road, and two porters had helped him into a cab and accompanied him to the hotel, where, on being put to bed, he again lapsed into unconsciousness. A doctor was called, but he could not diagnose the ailment, except that the patient's heart was seriously affected and, that being so, a fatal termination of the seizure might ensue. Towards two o'clock next morning, Blair, who had neither given his name nor told the hotel people who he was, asked that both Seton and I should be telegraphed for, and the result was that in anxious surprise we had both travelled up to Manchester, where on arrival, an hour before, we had discovered our friend to be in an utterly hopeless condition.

On entering the room we found the doctor, a young and rather pleasant man named Glenn, in attendance. Blair was conscious, and listened to the medical opinion without flinching. Indeed, he seemed rather to welcome death than to dread it, for, when he heard that he was in such a very critical condition, a faint smile crossed his pale, drawn features, and he remarked—

"Every man must die, so it may as well be to-day as to-morrow." Then, turning to me, he added, "Gilbert, you are very good to come just to say good-bye," and he put out his thin cold hand and grasped mine, while his eyes fixed upon me with that strange, intent look that only comes into a man's gaze when he is on the brink of the grave.

"It is a friend's duty, Burton," I answered, deeply in earnest. "But you must still hope. Doctors are often mistaken. Why, you've a splendid constitution, haven't you?"

"Hardly ever had a day's illness since I was a kid," was the millionaire's reply in a low, weak voice; "but this fit has bowled me completely over."

We endeavoured to ascertain exactly how he was seized, but neither Reggie not the doctor could gather anything tangible.

"I became faint all of a sudden, and I know nothing more," was all the dying man would reply. "But," he added, turning again to me, "don't tell Mab till it's all over. Poor girl! My only regret is to leave her. You two fellows were so very good to her back in the old days, you won't abandon her now, will you?" he implored, speaking slowly and with very great difficulty, tears standing in his eyes.

"Certainly not, old chap," was my answer. "If left alone she'll want some one to advise her and to look after her interests."

"The scoundrelly lawyer chaps will do that," he snapped, with a strange hardness in his voice, as though he entertained no love for his solicitors. "No, I want you to see that no man marries her for her money—you understand? Dozens of fellows are after her at this moment, I know, but I'd rather see her dead than she should marry one of them. She must marry for love—love, you hear? Promise me, Gilbert, that that you'll look after her, won't you?"

Still holding his hand, I promised.

That was the last word he uttered. His pale lips twitched again, but no sound came from them. His glassy eyes were fixed upon me with a stony, terrible stare, as though he were endeavouring to tell me something.

Perhaps he was revealing to me the great secret—the secret of how he had solved the mystery of fortune and become worth over a million sterling—perhaps he was speaking of Mab. Which we knew not. His tongue refused to articulate, the silence of death was upon him.

Thus he passed away; and thus did I find myself bound to a promise which I intended to fulfil, even though he had not revealed to us his secret, as we confidently expected. We believed that, knowing himself to be dying, he had summoned us there to impart that knowledge which would render us both rich beyond the dreams of avarice. But in this we had been most bitterly disappointed. For five years, I confess, we had waited, expecting that he would some day share some of his wealth with us in return for those services we had rendered him in the past. Yet now it seemed he had coolly disregarded his indebtedness to us, and at the same time imposed upon me a duty by no means easy— the guardianship of his only daughter Mabel.

II

Contains Certain Mysterious Facts

I ought here to declare that, having regard to all the curious and mysterious circumstances of the past, the situation was, to me, far from satisfactory. As we strolled together along Market Street that cold night discussing the affair, rather than remain in the public room of the hotel, Reggie suggested that the secret might be written somewhere and sealed up among the dead man's effects. But in that case, unless it were addressed to us, it would be opened by the persons the dying man had designated as "those scoundrelly lawyer chaps," and in all probability be turned by them to profitable account.

His solicitors were, we knew, Messrs. Leighton, Brown and Leighton, an eminently respectable firm in Bedford Row; therefore we sent a telegram from the Central Office informing them of their client's sudden death, and requesting that one of the firm should at once come to Manchester to attend the inquest which Doctor Glenn had declared would be necessary. As the deceased man had expressed a wish that Mabel should, for the present, remain in ignorance, we did not inform her of the tragic occurrence.

Curiosity prompted us to ascend again to the dead man's chamber and examine the contents of his kit-bag and suit-case, but, beyond his clothes, a cheque-book and about ten pounds in gold, we found nothing. I think that we both half expected to discover the key to that remarkable secret which he had somehow obtained, yet it was hardly to be imagined that he would carry such a valuable asset about with him in his luggage.

In the pocket of a small writing-book which formed part of the fittings of the suit-case I discovered several letters, all of which I examined and found them to be of no importance—save one, a dirty, ill-written note in uneducated Italian, which contained some passages which struck me as curious.

Indeed, so strange was the tenor of the whole communication that, with Reggie's connivance, I resolved to take possession of it and make further inquiry.

There were many things about Burton Blair that had puzzled us for years, therefore we were both determined, if possible, to elucidate the curious mystery that had surrounded him, even if he had carried to his grave the secret of his enormous fortune.

We alone in all the world knew the existence of the secret, only we were in ignorance of the necessary key by which the source of riches could be opened. The manner in which he had gained his great wealth was a mystery to every one, even to his daughter Mabel. In the City and in Society he was vaguely believed by some to possess large interests in mines, and to be a successful speculator in stocks, while others declared that he was the ground-landlord of at least two large cities in America, and yet others were positive that certain concessions from the Ottoman Government had brought him his gold.

All were, however, mistaken in their surmises. Burton Blair possessed not an acre of land; he had not a shilling in any public company; he was not interested in either Government concessions or industrial enterprises. No. The source of the great wealth by which he had, in five years, been able to purchase, decorate and furnish in princely manner one of the finest houses in Grosvenor Square, keep three of the most expensive Panhards, motoring being his hobby, and rent that fine old Jacobean mansion Mayvill Court, in Herefordshire, came from a source which nobody knew or even suspected. His were mysterious millions.

"I wonder if anything will come out at the inquest?" queried Reggie, later that evening. "His lawyers undoubtedly know nothing."

"He may have left some paper which reveals the truth," I answered. "Men who are silent in life often commit their secrets to paper."

"I don't think Burton ever did."

"He may have done so for Mabel's benefit, remember."

"Ah! by Jove!" gasped my friend, "I never thought of that. If he wished to provide for her, he would leave his secret with some one whom he could implicitly trust. Yet he trusted us—up to a certain point. We are the only ones who have any real knowledge of the state of affairs," and my tall, long-legged, fair-haired friend, who stood six feet in his stockings, the picture of the easygoing muscular Englishman, although engaged in the commerce of feminine frippery, stopped with a low grunt of dissatisfaction, and carefully lit a fresh cigar.

We passed a dismal evening strolling about the main streets of Manchester, feeling that in Burton Blair we had lost a friend, but when on the following morning we met Herbert Leighton, the solicitor, in the hall of the *Queen's*, and had a long consultation with him, the mystery surrounding the dead man became considerably heightened.

"You both knew my late client very well, indeed," the solicitor remarked, after some preliminaries. "Now, are you aware of the existence of any one who would profit by his sudden decease?"

"That's a curious question," I remarked. "Why?"

"Well, the fact is this," explained the dark, sharp-featured man, with some hesitation. "I have every reason to believe that he has been the victim of foul play."

"Foul play!" I gasped. "You surely don't think that he was murdered? Why, my dear fellow, that couldn't be. He was taken ill in the train, and died in bed in our presence."

The solicitor, whose face had now become graver, merely shrugged his narrow shoulders, and said—"We must, of course, await the result of the inquest, but from information in my possession I feel confident that Burton Blair did not die a natural death."

That same evening the Coroner held his inquiry in a private room in the hotel, and, according to the two doctors who had made the postmortem earlier in the day, death was due entirely to natural causes. It was discovered that Blair had naturally a weak heart, and that the fatal termination had been accelerated by the oscillation of the train.

There was absolutely nothing whatever to induce any suspicion of foul play, therefore the jury returned a verdict in accordance with the medical evidence that death was due to natural causes, and an order was given for the removal of the body to London for burial.

An hour after the inquest I took Mr. Leighton aside and said—

"As you know, I have for some years been one of the late Mr. Blair's most intimate friends, and, therefore, I am naturally very much interested to know what induced you to suspect foul play."

"My suspicions were well based," was his rather enigmatical answer.

"Upon what?"

"Upon the fact that my client himself had been threatened, and that, although he told no one and laughed at my suggested precautions, he has lived in daily dread of assassination."

"Curious!" I exclaimed. "Very curious!"

I told him nothing of that remarkable letter I had secured from the dead man's luggage. If what he said were really true, then there was a very extraordinary secret in the death of Burton Blair, equally with that of his strange, romantic and mysterious life—a secret that was inscrutable, yet absolutely unique.

It will be necessary, I think, to fully explain the curious circumstances which first brought us into contact with Burton Blair, and to describe the mysterious events which followed our acquaintanceship. From beginning to end the whole affair is so remarkable that many who read this record of facts may be inclined to doubt my veracity. To such, I would at the very outset suggest that they make inquiries in London, in that little world of adventurers, speculators, money-lenders and money-losers known as "the City," where I feel sure they will have no difficulty in learning even further interesting details regarding the man of mysterious millions whom this narrative partially concerns.

And certainly the true facts concerning him will, I do not hesitate to say, be found to form one of the most remarkable romances in modern life.

III

In which a Strange Story is Told

In order to put the plain, unvarnished truth before you, I must, in the first place, explain that I, Gilbert Greenwood, was a man of small means, having been left an annuity by an ascetic Baptist, but somewhat prosperous aunt, while Reginald Seton I had known ever since we had been lads together at Charterhouse. The son of George Seton, a lace warehouseman of Cannon Street and Alderman of the City of London, Reggie had been left at twenty-five with a heavy burden of debt and an old-fashioned, high-class but rapidly declining business. Still, brought up to the lace trade in a factory at Nottingham, Reggie boldly followed in his father's footsteps, and by dint of close attention to business succeeding in rubbing along sufficiently well to avoid the bankruptcy court, and to secure an income of a few hundreds a year.

Both of us were still bachelors, and we chummed in comfortable chambers in a newly-constructed block of flats in Great Russell Street, while, being also fond of fox-hunting, the only sport we could afford, we also rented a cheap, old-fashioned house in a rural village called Helpstone, eighty miles from London, in the Fitzwilliam country. Here we spent each winter, usually being "out" two days a week.

Neither of us being well off, we had, as may be imagined, to practise a good deal of economy, for fox-hunting is an expensive sport to the poor man. Nevertheless, we were both fortunate in possessing a couple of good horses apiece, and by dint of a little squeezing here and there, were able to indulge in those exhilarating runs across country which cause the blood to tingle with excitement, and rejuvenate all who take part in them.

Reggie was sometimes kept in town by the exigencies of his deal in torchon, Maltese and Honiton, therefore I frequently lived alone in the old-fashioned, ivy-covered house, with Glave, my man, to look after me.

One bitterly cold evening in January Reggie was absent in London, and I, having been hunting all day, was riding home utterly fagged out. The meet that morning had been at Kate's Cabin, over in Huntingdonshire, and after two good runs I had found myself beyond Stilton, eighteen miles from home. Still, the scent had been excellent, and we had had good sport, therefore I took a pull at my flask and rode forward across country in the gathering gloom.

Fortunately I found the river fordable at Water Newton mill, a fact which saved me the long detour by Wansford, and then when within a mile of home I allowed my horse to walk, as I always did, in order that he might cool down before going to his stable. The dusk of the short afternoon was just deepening into night, and the biting wind cut me like a knife as I passed the crossroads about half a mile from Helpstone village, jogging along steadily, when of a sudden a man's burly figure loomed out of the shadow of the high, holly hedge, and a deep voice exclaimed—

"Pardon me, sir, but I'm a stranger in these parts, and my daughter here has fainted. Is there a house near?"

Then, as I drew near, I saw huddled upon a heap of stones at the roadside the slim, fragile form of a young girl of about sixteen, wrapped in a thick, dark-coloured cloak, while in the glimmer of light that remained I distinguished that the man who was addressing me was a bluff, rather well-spoken, dark-bearded fellow of about forty-five or so, in a frayed suit of blue serge and peaked cap that gave him something of the appearance of a seafarer. His face was seamed and weatherbeaten, and his broad, powerful jaws betokened a strength of character and dogged determination.

"Has your daughter been taken ill?" I inquired, when I had thoroughly examined him.

"Well, the fact is we've walked a long way to-day, and I think she's done up. She became dazed like about half an hour ago, and when she sat down she fell insensible."

"She mustn't stay here," I remarked, as the fact became plain that both father and daughter were tramps. "She'll get frozen to death. My house is over yonder. I'll ride on and bring back some one to help carry her."

The man commenced to thank me, but I touched my horse with the spur, and was soon in the stableyard calling for Glave to accompany me back to the spot where I had left the wayfarers.

A quarter of an hour later we had arranged the insensible girl on a couch in my warm, snug sitting-room, had forced some brandy down her throat, and she had opened her eyes wonderingly, and looked round with childlike temerity upon her unfamiliar surroundings.

Her gaze met mine, and I saw that her countenance was undeniably beautiful, of that dark, half-tragic type, her eyes rendered the more luminous by the death-like pallor of her countenance. The features were well-moulded, refined and handsome in every line, and as she addressed her father, inquiring what had occurred, I detected that she was no mere waif of the highway, but, on the contrary, highly intelligent, well mannered and well educated.

Her father, in a few deep words, explained our abrupt meeting and my hospitality, whereupon she smiled upon me sweetly and uttered words of thanks.

"It must have been the intense cold, I think," she added. "Somehow I felt benumbed all at once, and my head swam so that I couldn't stand. But it is really very kind indeed of you. I'm so sorry that we've disturbed you like this."

I assured her that my only wish was for her complete recovery, and as I spoke I could not conceal from myself that her beauty was very remarkable. Although young, and her figure as yet not fully developed, her face was nevertheless one of the most perfect I had ever seen. From the first moment my eyes fell upon her, I found her indescribably charming. That she was utterly exhausted was rendered plain by the painful, uneasy manner in which she moved upon her couch. Her rusty black skirt and thick boots were muddy and travel-stained, and by the manner she pushed the tangled mass of dark hair from her brow I knew that her head ached.

Glave, in no good mood at the introduction of tramps, entered, announcing that my dinner was ready; but she firmly, yet with sweet grace, declined my invitation to eat, saying that if I would permit her she would rather remain alone on the couch before the fire for half an hour longer. Therefore I sent her some hot soup by old Mrs. Axford, our cook, while her father, having washed his hands, accompanied me to the diningroom.

He seemed half-famished, taciturn and reserved at first, but presently, when he had judged my character sufficiently, he explained that his name was Burton Blair, that in his absence abroad he had lost his wife ten years before, and that little Mab was his only child. As his appearance denoted, he had been at sea the greater part of his life and held a master's certificate, but of late he had been living ashore.

"I've been home these three years now," he went on, "and I've had a pretty rough time of it, I can tell you. Poor Mab! I wouldn't have minded had it not been for her. She's a brick, she is, just as her poor dear mother was. She's done three years of semi-starvation, and yet she's never once complained. She knows my character by now, she knows that when once Burton Blair makes up his mind to do a thing, by Gad! he does it," and he set those square jaws of his hard, while a look of determination and dogged persistency came into his eyes, the fiercest I had ever seen in any man.

"But, Mr. Blair, why did you leave the sea to starve ashore?" I inquired, my curiosity aroused.

"Because—well, because I had a reason—a strong reason," was his hesitating reply. "You see me homeless and hungry to-night," laughed Burton Blair, bitterly, "but to-morrow I may be a millionaire!"

And his face assumed a mysterious, sphinx-like expression which sorely puzzled me.

Many and many a time since then have I recollected those strange, prophetic words of his as he sat at my table, shabby, unkempt and ravenously hungry, a worn-out, half-frozen tramp from the highroad, who, absurd as it then seemed, held the strong belief that ere long he would be the possessor of millions.

I remember well how I smiled at his vague assertion. Every man who falls low in the social scale clings to the will-o'-the-wisp belief that his luck will change, and that by some vagary of fortune he will come up again smiling. Hope is never dead within the ruined man.

By dint of some careful questions I tried to obtain further information regarding this confident hope of wealth which he entertained, but he would tell me nothing—absolutely nothing.

He accepted a cigar after he had dined well, took brandy with his coffee, and smoked with the air of a contented man who had no single thought or care in the world—a man who knew exactly what the future held for him.

Thus, from the very first, Burton Blair was a mystery. On rejoining Mabel we found her sleeping peacefully, utterly fagged out. Therefore I induced him to remain beneath my roof that night, in order that she might rest, and, returning to the dining-room, her father and I sat together smoking and talking for several hours.

He told me of his hard, rough years at sea, of strange adventures in savage lands, of a narrow escape from death at the hands of a band of natives in the Cameroons, and of how, for three years, he acted as captain of a river-steamer up the Congo, one of the pioneers of civilisation. He related his thrilling adventures calmly and naturally, without any bragging, but just in that plain, matter-of-fact manner which revealed to me that he was one of those men who love an adventurous life because of its perils and its vicissitudes.

"And now I'm tramping the turnpikes of England," he added, laughing. "You must, no doubt, think it very strange, Mr. Greenwood, but to tell you the truth I am actively prosecuting a rather curious quest, the successful issue of which will one day bring me wealth beyond my wildest dreams. See!" he added, with a strange wild look in his great dark eyes, as swiftly undoing his blue guernsey and delving beneath it he drew forth a square, flat piece of soiled and well-worn chamois leather in which there seemed to be sewed some precious document or other. "Look! My secret lies here. Some day I shall discover the key to it—maybe to-morrow or next day, or next year. When, it is quite immaterial. The result will be the same. My years of continuous search and travel will be rewarded—and I shall be rich, and the world will wonder!" And, laughing contentedly, almost triumphantly within himself, he carefully replaced his precious document in his chest, and, rising, stood with his back to the fire in the attitude of a man entirely confident of what was written in the Book of Fate.

That midnight scene in all its strange, romantic detail, that occasion when the tired wayfarer and his daughter spent their first night as my guests, rose before me when, on that bright, cold afternoon following the inquest up at Manchester, I alighted from a cab in front of the big white house in Grosvenor Square, and received word of Carter, the solemn manservant, that Miss Mabel was at home.

The magnificent mansion, with its exquisite decorations, its genuine Louis Quatorze furniture, its valuable pictures and splendid examples of seventeenth century statuary, home of one to whom expense was surely of no account, was assuredly sufficient testimony that the shabby wayfarer who had uttered those words in my narrow little dining-room five years before had made no idle boast.

The secret sewed within that dirty bag of wash-leather, whatever it may have been, had already realised over a million, and was still realising enormous sums, until death had now so suddenly put an end to its exploitation. The mystery of it all was beyond solution; and the enigma was complete.

These and other reflections swept through my mind as I followed the footman up the wide marble staircase and was shown ceremoniously into the great gold and white drawing-room, the walls of which were panelled with pale rose silk, the four large windows affording a wide view across the Square. Those priceless paintings, those beautiful cabinets and unique *bric-a-brac*—all were purchased with the proceeds from that mysterious secret, the secret which had in that short space of five years been the means of transforming a homeless, down-at-heel wanderer into a millionaire.

Gazing aimlessly across the grey Square with its leafless trees, I stood undecided how best to break the sad news, when a slight *frou-frou* of silk swept behind me, and, turning quickly, I confronted the dead man's daughter, looking now, at twenty-three, far more sweet, graceful and womanly than in that first hour of our strange meeting by the wayside long ago.

But her black gown, her trembling form, and her pale, tear-stained cheeks told me in an instant that this woman in my charge had already learnt the painful truth. She halted before me, a beautiful, tragic figure, her tiny white hand nervously clutching the back of one of the gilt chairs for support.

"I know!" she exclaimed in a broken voice, quite unnatural to her, her eyes fixed upon me, "I know, Mr. Greenwood, why you have called. The truth has been told to me by Mr. Leighton an hour ago. Ah! my poor dear father!" she sighed, the words catching in her throat as she burst into tears. "Why did he go to Manchester? His enemies have triumphed, just as I have all along feared they would. Yet, great-hearted as he was, he believed ill of no man. He refused always to heed my warnings, and laughed at all my apprehensions. Yet, alas! the ghastly truth is now only too plain. My poor father!" she gasped, her handsome face blanched to the lips. "He is dead—and his secret is out!"

IV

Which Traverses Dangerous Ground

"A re you really suspicious, Mabel, that your father has been the victim of foul play?" I inquired quickly of the dead man's daughter, standing pale and unnerved before me.

"I am," was her direct, unhesitating answer. "You know his story, Mr. Greenwood; you know how he carried with him everywhere something he had sewed in a piece of chamois leather; something which was his most precious possession. Mr. Leighton tells me that it is missing."

"That is unfortunately so," I said. "We all three searched for it among his clothes and in his luggage; we made inquiry of the luncheon-car attendant who found him insensible in the railway carriage, of the porters who conveyed him to the hotel, of every one, in fact, but can find no trace of it whatsoever."

"Because it has been deliberately stolen," she remarked.

"Then your theory is that he has been assassinated in order to conceal the theft?"

She nodded in the affirmative, her face still hard and pale.

"But there is no evidence whatever of foul play, recollect," I exclaimed. "Both medical men, two of the best in Manchester, declared that death was entirely due to natural causes."

"I care nothing for what they say. The little sachet which my poor father sewed with his own hands, and guarded so carefully all these years, and which for some curious reason he would neither trust in any bank nor in a safe deposit vault, is missing. His enemies have gained possession of it, just as I felt confident they would."

"I recollect him showing me that little bag of wash-leather on the first night of our acquaintance," I said. "He then declared that what was contained therein would bring him wealth—and it certainly has done," I added, glancing round that magnificent apartment.

"It brought him wealth, but not happiness, Mr. Greenwood," she responded quickly. "That packet, the contents of which I have never seen, he has carried with him in his pocket or suspended round his neck ever since it first came into his possession years ago. In all his clothes he had a special pocket in which to carry it, while at night he wore it in a specially made belt which was locked around his waist. I think he regarded it as a sort of charm, or talisman, which, besides bringing him his great fortune, also preserved him from all ills. The reason of this I cannot tell."

"Did you never ascertain the nature of the document which he considered so precious?"

"I tried to do so many times, but he would never reveal it to me. 'It was his secret,' he would say, and no more."

Both Reggie and I had, times without number, endeavoured to learn what the mysterious packet really contained, but had been no more successful than the charming girl now standing before me. Burton Blair was a strange man, both in actions and in words, very reserved regarding his own affairs, and yet, curiously enough, with the advent of prosperity he had become a prince of good fellows.

"But who were his enemies?" I inquired.

"Ah! of that I am likewise in utter ignorance," was her reply. "As you know, during the past year or two, like all rich men he has been surrounded by adventurers and parasites of all sorts, whom Ford, his secretary, has kept at arm's length. It may be that the existence of the precious packet was known, and that my poor father has fallen a victim to some foul plot. At least, that is my firm idea."

"If so, the police should certainly be informed," I said. "It is true that the wash-leather sachet which he showed me on the night of our first meeting is now missing, for we have all made the most careful search for it, but in vain. Yet what could its possession possibly profit any one if the key to what was contained there is wanting?"

"But was not this key, whatever it was, also in my father's hands?" queried Mabel Blair. "Was it not the discovery of that very key which gave us all these possessions?" she asked, with the sweet womanliness that was her most engaging characteristic.

"Exactly. But surely your father, shrewd and cautious as he always was, would never carry upon his person both problem and key together! I can't really believe that he'd do such a foolish thing as that."

"Nor do I. Although I was his only child, and his confidante in everything relating to his life, there was one thing he persistently kept from me, and that was the nature of his secret. Sometimes I have found myself suspecting that it was not an altogether creditable one—indeed, one that a father dare not reveal to his daughter. And yet no

WILLIAM LE QUEUX

one has ever accused him of dishonesty or of double-dealing. At other times I have noticed in his face and manner an air of distinct mystery which has caused me to believe that the source of our unlimited wealth was some curious and romantic one, which to the world would be regarded as entirely incredible. One night, indeed, as we sat here at table after dinner, and while smoking, he had been telling me about my poor mother who died in lodgings in a back street in Manchester while he was absent on a voyage to the West Coast of Africa, he declared that if London knew the source of his income it would be astounded. 'But,' he added, 'it is a secret—a secret I intend to carry with me to the grave.'"

Strangely enough he had uttered those very same words to me a couple of years before, when one night he had sat before the fire in my rooms in Great Russell Street, and I had referred to his marvellous stroke of good fortune. He had died, and he had either carried out his threat of destroying that evidence of his secret in the shape of the well-worn chamois leather bag, or else it had been ingeniously stolen from him.

The curious, ill-written letter I had secured from my friend's luggage, while puzzling me had aroused certain suspicions that hitherto I had not entertained. Of these I, of course, told Mabel nothing, for I did not wish to cause her any greater pain. In the years we had been acquainted we had always been good friends. Although Reggie was fifteen years her senior, and I thirteen years older than she, I believe she regarded both of us as big brothers.

Our friendship had commenced when, finding Burton Blair, the seafaring tramp, practically-starving as he was, we clubbed together from our small means and put her to a finishing school at Bournemouth. To allow so young and delicate a girl to tramp England aimlessly in search of some vague and secret information which seemed to be her erratic father's object, was, we decided, an utter impossibility; therefore, following that night of our first meeting at Helpstone, Burton and his daughter remained our guests for a week, and, after many consultations and some little economies, we were at last successful in placing Mabel at school, a service for which we later received her heartfelt thanks.

She was utterly worn out, poor child. Poverty had already set its indelible stamp upon her sweet face, and her beauty was beginning to fade beneath that burden of disappointment and erratic wandering when we had so fortunately discovered her, and been able to rescue her from the necessity of tramping footsore over those endless, pitiless highways.

Contrary to our expectation it was quite a long time before we could induce Blair to allow his daughter to return to school, for, as a matter of fact, both father and daughter were entirely devoted to one another. Nevertheless, in the end we triumphed, and later, when the bluff, bearded wayfarer came to his own, he did not forget to return thanks to us in a very substantial manner. Indeed, our present improved circumstances were due to him, for not only had he handed a cheque to Reggie sufficient to pay the whole of the liabilities of the Cannon Street lace business, but to me, on my birthday three years ago, he had sent, enclosed in a cheap, silver cigarette case, a draft upon his bankers for a sum sufficient to provide me with a very comfortable little annuity.

Burton Blair never forgot his friends—neither did he ever forgive an unkind action. Mabel was his idol, his only real confidante, and yet it seemed more than strange that she knew absolutely nothing of the mysterious source of his colossal income.

Together we sat for over an hour in that great drawing-room, the very splendour of which spoke mystery. Mrs. Percival, the pleasant, middle-aged widow of a naval surgeon, who was Mabel's chaperon and companion, entered, but left us quickly, much upset by the tragic news. Presently, when I told Mabel of my promise to her father, a slight blush suffused her pale cheeks.

"It is really awfully good of you to trouble over my affairs, Mr. Greenwood," she said, glancing at me, and then dropping her eyes modestly. "I suppose in future I shall have to consider you as my guardian," and she laughed lightly, twisting her ring around her finger.

"Not as your legal guardian," I answered. "Your father's lawyers will, no doubt, act in that capacity, but rather as your protector and your friend."

"Ah!" she replied sadly, "I suppose I shall require both, now that poor dad is dead."

"I have been your friend for over five years, Mabel, and I hope you will still allow me to carry out my promise to your father," I said, standing before her and speaking in deep earnestness.

"There must, however, at the outset be a clear and distinct understanding between us. Therefore permit me for one moment to speak to you candidly, as a man should to a woman who is his friend.

You, Mabel, are young, and—well, you are, as you know, very good-looking—"

"No, really, Mr. Greenwood," she cried, interrupting me and blushing at my compliment, "it is too bad of you. I'm sure—"

"Hear me out, please," I continued with mock severity. "You are young, you are very good-looking, and you are rich; you therefore possess the three necessary attributes which render a woman eligible in these modern days when sentiment is held of such little account. Well, people who will watch our intimate friendship will, with ill-nature, declare, no doubt, that I am seeking to marry you for your money. I am quite sure the world will say this, but what I want you to promise is to at once refute such a statement. I desire that you and I shall be firm friends, just as we have ever been, without any thought of affection. I may admire you—I confess, now, that I have always admired you—but with a man of my limited means love for you is entirely out of the question. Understand that I do not wish to presume upon the past, now that your father is dead and you are alone. Understand, too, from the very outset that I now give you the hand of firm friendship as I would give it to Reggie, my old schoolfellow and best friend, and that in future I shall safeguard your interests as though they were my own." And I held out my hands to her.

For a moment she hesitated, for my words had apparently caused her the most profound surprise.

"Very well," she faltered, glancing for an instant up to my face. "It is a bargain—if you wish it to be so."

"I wish, Mabel, to carry out the promise I made to your father," I said. "As you know, I am greatly indebted to him for much generosity, and I wish, therefore, as a mark of gratitude, to stand in his place and protect his daughter—yourself."

"But were we not, in the first place, both indebted to you?" she said. "If it had not been for Mr. Seton and yourself I might have wandered on until I died by the wayside."

"For what was your father searching?" I asked. "He surely told you?"

"No, he never did. I am in entire ignorance of the reason of his three years of tramping up and down England. He had a distinct object, which he accomplished, but what it actually was he would never reveal to me."

"It was, I suppose, in connexion with that document he always carried?"

"I believe it was," was her response. Then she added, returning to her previous observations, "Why speak of your indebtedness to him, Mr. Greenwood, when I know full well how you sold your best horse in order to pay my school fees at Bournemouth, and that you could not hunt that season in consequence? You denied yourself the only little pleasure you had, in order that I might be well cared for."

"I forbid you to mention that again," I said quickly. "Recollect we are now friends, and between friends there can be no question of indebtedness."

"Then you must not talk of any little service my father rendered to you," she laughed. "Come, now, I shall be unruly if you don't keep to your part of the bargain!"

And so we were compelled at that juncture to cry quits, and we recommenced our friendship on a firm and perfectly well-defined basis.

Yet how strange it was! The beauty of Mabel Blair, as she lounged there before me in that magnificent home that was now hers, was surely sufficient to turn the head of any man who was not a Chancery Judge or a Catholic Cardinal—different indeed from the poor, half-starved girl whom I had first seen exhausted and fallen by the roadside in the winter gloom.

V

In which the Mystery Becomes Considerably Increased

That the precious document, or whatever it was, sewn up in the wash-leather which the dead man had so carefully guarded through all those years was now missing was, in itself, a very suspicious circumstance, while Mabel's vague but distinct apprehensions, which she either would not or could not define, now aroused my suspicions that Burton Blair had been the victim of foul play.

Immediately after leaving her I therefore drove to Bedford Row and held another consultation with Leighton, to whom I explained my grave fears.

"As I have already explained, Mr. Greenwood," responded the solicitor, leaning back in his padded chair and regarding me gravely through his glasses, "I believe that my client did not die a natural death. There was some mystery in his life, some strange romantic circumstance which, unfortunately, he never thought fit to confide to me. He held a secret, he told me, and by knowledge of that secret, he obtained his vast wealth. Only half an hour ago I made a rough calculation of the present value of his estate, and at the lowest, I believe it will be found to amount to over two and a half millions. The whole of this, I may tell you in confidence, goes unreservedly to his daughter, with the exception of several legacies, which include ten thousand each to Mr. Seton and to yourself, two thousand to Mrs. Percival, and some small sums to the servants. But," he added, "there is a clause in the will which is very puzzling, and which closely affects yourself. As we both suspect foul play, I think I may as well at once show it to you without waiting for my unfortunate client's burial and the formal reading of his will."

Then he rose, and from a big black deed box lettered "Burton Blair, Esquire," he took out the dead man's will, and, opening it, showed me a passage which read:—

Ten: "I give and bequeath to Gilbert Greenwood of The Cedars, Helpstone, the small bag of chamois leather that will be found upon me at the time of my death, in order that he may profit by what is contained therein, and as recompense for certain valuable services rendered to me. Let him recollect always this rhyme—

"*Henry the Eighth was a knave to his queens, He'd, one short of seven— and nine or ten scenes!*'

"And let him well and truly preserve the secret from every man, just as I have done."

That was all. A strange clause surely! Burton Blair had, after all, actually bequeathed his secret to me, the secret that had brought him his colossal wealth! Yet it was already lost—probably stolen by his enemies.

"That's a curious doggerel," the solicitor smiled. "But poor Blair possessed but little literary culture, I fear. He knew more about the sea than poetry. Yet, after all, it seems a tantalising situation that you should be left the secret of the source of my client's enormous fortune, and that it should be stolen from you in this manner."

"We had, I think, better consult the police, and explain our suspicions," I said, in bitter chagrin that the chamois sachet should have fallen into other hands.

"I entirely agree with you, Mr. Greenwood. We will go together to Scotland Yard and get them to institute inquiries. If Mr. Blair was actually murdered, then his assassination was accomplished in a most secret and remarkable manner, to say the least. But there is one further clause in the will which is somewhat disturbing, and that is with regard to his daughter Mabel. The testator has appointed some person of whom I have never heard—a man called Paolo Melandrini, an Italian, apparently living in Florence, to be her secretary and the manager of her affairs."

"What!" I cried, amazed. "An Italian to be her secretary! Who is he?"

"A person with whom I am not acquainted; whose name, indeed, has never been mentioned to me by my client. He merely dictated it to me when I drafted the will."

"But the thing's absurd!" I exclaimed. "Surely you can't let an unknown foreigner, who may be an adventurer for all we know, have control of all her money?"

"I fear there's no help for it," replied Leighton, gravely. "It is written here, and we shall be compelled to give notice to this man, whoever he is, of his appointment at a salary of five thousand pounds a year."

"And will he really have control of her affairs?"

"Absolutely. Indeed, the whole estate is left to her on condition that she accepts this fellow as her secretary and confidential adviser."

"Why, Blair must have been mad!" I exclaimed. "Has Mabel any knowledge of this mysterious Italian?"

"She has never heard of him."

"Well, in that case, I think that, before he is informed of poor Blair's death and the good fortune in store for him, we ought at least to find out who and what he is. We can in any case, keep a watchful eye on him, and see that he doesn't trick Mabel out of her money."

The lawyer sighed, wiped his glasses slowly, and said—

"He will have the entire management of everything, therefore it will be difficult to know what goes on, or how much he puts into his own pocket."

"But whatever could possess Blair to insert such a mad clause as that? Didn't you point out the folly of it?"

"I did."

"And what did he say?"

"He reflected a few moments over my words, sighed, and then answered, 'It is imperative, Leighton. I have no other alternative.' Therefore from that I took it that he was acting under compulsion."

"You believe that this foreigner was in a position to demand it—eh?"

The solicitor nodded. He evidently was of opinion that the reason of the introduction of this unknown person into Mabel's household was a secret one, known only to Burton Blair and to the individual himself. It was curious, I reflected, that Mabel herself had not mentioned it to me. Yet perhaps she had hesitated, because I had told her of my promise to her father, and she did not wish to hurt my feelings. The whole situation became hourly more complicated and more mysterious.

I was, however, bent upon accomplishing two things; first, to recover the millionaire's most precious possession which he had bequeathed to me, together with such an extraordinary injunction to recollect that doggerel couplet which still ran in my head; and secondly, to make private inquiries regarding this unknown foreigner who had so suddenly become introduced into the affair.

That same evening at six o'clock, having met Reggie by appointment at Mr. Leighton's office, we all three drove to Scotland Yard, where we had a long consultation with one of the head officials, to whom we explained the circumstances and our suspicions of foul play.

"Well," he replied at length, "of course I will institute inquiries in Manchester and elsewhere, but as the medical evidence has proved so conclusively that the gentleman in question died from natural causes, I cannot hold out very much hope that out Department or the Manchester Detective Department can assist you. The grounds you have for supposing that he met with foul play are very vague, you must admit, and as far as I can see, the only motive at all was the theft of this paper, or whatever it was, which he carried upon him. Yet men are not usually killed in broad daylight in order to commit a theft which any expert pickpocket might effect. Besides, if his enemies or rivals knew what it was and how he was in the habit of carrying it, they could easily have secured it without assassination."

"But he was in possession of some secret," remarked the solicitor.

"Of what character?"

"I have unfortunately no idea. Nobody knows. All that we are aware is that its possession raised him from poverty to affluence, and that one person, if not more, was eager to obtain possession of it."

"Naturally," remarked the grey-haired Assistant-Director of Criminal Investigations. "But who was this person?"

"Unfortunately I do not know. My client told me this a year ago, but mentioned no name."

"Then you have no suspicion whatever of any one?"

"None. The little bag of wash leather, inside which the document was sewn, has been stolen, and this fact arouses our suspicion of foul play." The hide-bound official shook his head very dubiously.

"That is not enough upon which to base a suspicion of murder, especially as we have had all the evidence at the inquest, a post-mortem and a unanimous verdict of the coroner's jury. No, gentlemen," he added, "I don't see any ground for really grave suspicion. The document may not have been stolen after all. Mr. Blair seems to have been of a somewhat eccentric disposition, like many men who suddenly rise in the world, and he may have hidden it away for safe-keeping somewhere. To me, this seems by far the most likely theory, especially as he had expressed a fear that his enemies sought to gain possession of it."

"But surely, if there is suspicion of murder, it is the duty of the police to investigate it!" I exclaimed resentfully.

"Granted. But where is the suspicion? Neither doctors, coroner, local police nor jury entertain the slightest doubt that he died from natural causes," he argued. "In that case the Manchester police have neither right nor necessity to interfere."

"But there has been a theft."

"What proof have you of it?" he asked, raising his grey eyebrows and tapping the table with his pen. "If you can show me that a theft has been committed, then I will put in motion the various influences at my command. On the contrary, you merely suspect that this something sewn in a bag has been stolen. Yet it may be hidden in some place difficult to find, but nevertheless in safety. As, however, you all three allege that the unfortunate gentleman was assassinated in order to gain possession of this mysterious little packet of which he was so careful, I will communicate with the Manchester City police and ask them to make what inquiries they can. Further than that, gentlemen," he added suavely, "I fear that my Department cannot assist you."

"Then all I have to reply," remarked Mr. Leighton, bluntly, "is that the public opinion of the futility of this branch of the police in the detection of crime is fully justified, and I shall not fail to see that public attention is called to the matter through the Press. It's simply a disgrace."

"I'm only acting, sir, upon my instructions, conjointly with what you have yourself told me," was his answer. "I assure you that if I ordered inquiries to be made in every case in which persons are alleged to have been murdered, I should require a detective force as large as the British Army. Why, not a day passes without I receive dozens of secret callers and anonymous letters all alleging assassination—generally against some person towards whom they entertain a dislike. Eighteen years as head of this Department, however, has, I think, taught me how to distinguish a case for inquiry—which yours is not."

Argument proved futile. The official mind was made up that Burton Blair had not fallen a victim to foul play, therefore we could hope for no assistance. So with our dissatisfaction rather plainly marked, we rose and went out again into Whitehall.

"It's a scandal!" Reggie declared angrily. "Poor Blair has been murdered—everything points to it—and yet the police won't lift a finger to assist us to reveal the truth, just because a doctor discovered that he had a weak heart. It's placing a premium on crime," he added, his fist clenched savagely. "I'll relate the whole thing to my friend Mills, the Member for West Derbyshire, and get him to ask a question in the House. We'll see what this new Home Secretary says to it! It'll be a nasty pill for him, I'll wager."

"Oh, he'll have some typewritten official excuse ready, never fear," laughed Leighton. "If they won't help us, we must make inquiries for ourselves."

The solicitor parted from us in Trafalgar Square, arranging to meet us at Grosvenor Square after the funeral, when the will would be formally read before the dead man's daughter and her companion, Mrs. Percival.

"And then," he added, "we shall have to take some active steps to discover this mysterious person who is in future to control her fortune."

"I'll undertake the inquiries," I said. "Fortunately I speak Italian, therefore, before we give him notice of Blair's death. I'll go out to Florence and ascertain who and what he is." Truth to tell, I had a suspicion that the letter which I had secured from the dead man's blotting book, and which I had kept secretly to myself, had been written by this unknown individual—Paolo Melandrini. Although it bore neither address nor signature, and was in a heavy and rather uneducated hand, it was evidently the letter of a Tuscan, for I detected in it certain phonetic spelling which was purely Florentine. Translated, the strange communication read as follows:—

"Your letter reached me only this morning. The Ceco (blind man) is in Paris, on his way to London. The girl is with him, and they evidently know something. So be very careful. He and his ingenious friends will probably try and trick you.

"I am still at my post, but the water has risen three metres on account of the heavy rains. Nevertheless, farming has been good, so I shall expect to meet you at vespers in San Frediano on the evening of the 6th of next month. I have something most important to tell you. Recollect that the Ceco means mischief, and act accordingly.

Addio

Times without number I carefully translated the curious missive word for word. It seemed full of hidden meaning.

What seemed most probable was that the person known as the "blind man," who was Blair's enemy, had actually been successful in gaining possession of that precious little sachet of chamois leather that was now mine by right, together with the mysterious secret it contained.

VI

Concerns Three Capital A's

The function in the library at Grosvenor Square on the following afternoon was, as may be supposed, a very sad and painful one.

Mabel Blair, dressed in deep mourning, her eyes betraying traces of tears, sat still and silent while the solicitor drily read over the will, clause by clause.

She made no comment, even when he repeated the dead man's appointment of the unknown Italian to be manager of his daughter's fortune.

"But who is he, pray?" demanded Mrs. Percival, in her quiet, refined voice. "I have never heard Mr. Blair speak of any such person."

"Nor have I," admitted Leighton, pausing a moment to readjust his glasses, and then continuing to read the document through to the end.

We were all thoroughly glad when the formality was over. Afterwards, Mabel whispered to me that she wished to see me alone in the morning-room, and when we had entered together and I had closed the door, she said—

"Last night I searched the small safe in my father's bedroom where he sometimes kept his private papers and things. There were a quantity of my poor mother's letters, written to him years ago when he was at sea, but nothing else, only this." And she drew from her pocket a small, soiled and frayed playing-card, an ace of hearts, upon which certain cabalistic capitals had been written in three columns. In order that you shall properly understand the arrangement and position of the letters, it will perhaps be as well if I here reproduce it:—

"That's curious!" I remarked, turning it over anxiously in my hand. "Have you tried to discover what meaning the words convey?"

"Yes; but it's some cipher or other, I think. You will notice that the two upper columns commence with 'A,' and the lower column ends with the same letter. The card is the ace of hearts, and in all those points I detect some hidden meaning."

"No doubt," I said. "But was there an appearance of it being carefully preserved?"

"Yes, it was sealed in a linen-lined envelope to itself, and marked in my father's handwriting, 'Burton Blair—private.' I wonder what it means?"

"Ah! I wonder," I exclaimed, pondering deeply, and still gazing upon the three columns of fourteen letters. I tried to decipher it by the usual known methods of the easy cipher, but could make nothing intelligible of it. There were some hidden words there, and being utterly unintelligible, they caused me considerable thought. Why Blair had preserved that card in such secrecy was, to say the least, a mystery. In it I suspected there was some hidden clue to his secret, but of its nature I could not even guess.

When we had discussed it for a long time, arriving at no satisfactory conclusion, I suggested that she should go abroad with Mrs. Percival for a few weeks so as to change her surroundings and endeavour to forget her sudden bereavement, but she only shook her head, murmuring—

"No, I prefer to remain here. The loss of my poor father would be the same to me abroad as it is here."

"But you must endeavour to forget," I urged with deep sympathy. "We are doing our utmost to solve the mystery surrounding your father's actions, and the means by which he came by his death. To-night, indeed, I am leaving for Italy in order to make secret inquiries regarding this person who is appointed your secretary."

"Ah, yes," she sighed. "I wonder who he is? I wonder what motive my father could possibly have in placing my affairs in the hands of a stranger?"

"He is probably an old friend of your father's," I suggested.

"No," she responded, "I knew all his friends. He had only one secret from me—the secret of the source of his wealth. That he always refused point blank to tell me."

"I shall travel direct to Florence, and discover what I can before the lawyers give this mysterious person notice of your father's death," I said. "I may obtain some knowledge which will be of the greatest benefit to us hereafter."

"Ah! it is really very good of you, Mr. Greenwood," she answered, lifting her beautiful eyes to mine with an expression of profound gratitude. "I must admit that the idea of being closely associated with a stranger, and that stranger a foreigner, causes me considerable apprehension."

"But he may be young and good looking, the veritable Paolo of romance—and you his Francesca," I suggested, smiling.

Her sweet lips relaxed slightly, but she shook her head, sighing as she answered—

"Please don't anticipate anything of the kind. I only hope he may be old and very ugly."

"So that he will not arouse my jealousy—eh?" I laughed. "Really, Mabel, if our friendship were not upon such a well-defined basis, I should allow myself to act the part of lover. You know I—"

"Now don't be foolish," she interrupted, raising her small finger in mock reproval. "Remember what you said yesterday."

"I said what I meant."

"And so did I. To tell you the truth, I like to think of you as my big brother," she declared. "I suppose I shall never love," she added, reflectively, gazing into the blazing fire.

"No, no; don't say that, Mabel. You'll one day meet some man in your own station, love him, marry and be happy," I said, my hand upon her shoulder. "Recollect that with your wealth you can secure the pick of the matrimonial market."

"Some impoverished young aristocrat, you mean? No, thanks. I've already met a good many, but their disguise of affection has always been much too thin. Most of them wanted my money to pay off mortgages on their estates. No, I'd much prefer a poor man—although I shall *never* marry—never."

I was silent for a moment, then I remarked quite bluntly—

"I always thought you would marry young Lord Newborough. You both seemed very good friends."

"So we were—until he proposed to me."

And she looked me straight in the face with that clear gaze and those splendid eyes wide open in wonderment, almost like a child's.

Her character was a strangely complex one. As a tall, willowy girl, in those early days of our acquaintance, I knew her to be high-minded and wilful, yet of that sweet affectionate disposition that endeared her to every one with whom she came into contact. Her nature was so calm and so sweet that in her love seemed an unconscious impulse. I had often thought she was surely too soft, too good, too fair to be cast among the briers of the world, and fall and bleed upon the thorns of life. The world is just as cold and pitiless and just as full of pitfalls for the young and unwary in Mayfair as in Mile End. Hence, to fulfil my promise to that man now silent in his grave, it was my duty to protect her from the thousand and one wiles of those who would endeavour to profit by sex and inexperience.

Her early privations, her hard life in youth while her father was absent at sea, and those weary months of tramping the turnpikes of England, all had had their effect upon her. With her, love seemed to be scarcely a passion or a sentiment, but a dreamy enchantment, a reverie which a fairy spell dissolved or riveted at pleasure. So exquisitely delicate was her character, just as was her countenance, that it seemed as if a touch would profane it. Like a strain of sad, sweet music which comes floating by on the wings of night and silence, and which we rather feel than hear, like the exhalation of the violet dying even upon the sense it charms, like the snow-flake dissolved in air before it has caught a stain of earth, like the light surf severed from the billow which a breath disperses—such was her nature, so full of that modesty, grace and tenderness without which a woman is no woman.

As she stood there before me, a frail, delicate figure in her plain black gown, and her hand in mine, thanking me for the investigation which I was undertaking in her behalf, and wishing me *bon voyage*, I shuddered to think of her thrown alone amid harsh and adverse destinies, and amid all the corruptions and sharks of society, perhaps without energy to resist, or will to act, or strength to endure. Alone in such a case, the end must inevitably be desolation.

I wished her farewell, turning from her with a feeling that, loving her as I admit I did, I was nevertheless unworthy of her. Yet surely I was playing a dangerous game!

I had entertained a strong and increasing affection for her ever since that winter's night down at Helpstone. Still, now that she was possessor of vast wealth, I felt that the difference in our ages and the fact that I was a poor man were both barriers to our marriage. Indeed, she had never exerted any of the feminine wiles of flirtation towards me; she had never once allowed me to think that I had captivated her. She had spoken the truth. She regarded me as an elder brother—that was all.

That same night, as I paced the deck of the Channel steamer in the teeth of a wintry gale, watching the revolving light of Calais harbour growing more and more distinct, my thoughts were full of her. Love is the teacher, grief the tamer, and time the healer of the human heart. While the engines throbbed, the wind howled and the dark seas swirled past, I paced up and down puzzling over the playing-card in my pocket and reflecting upon all that had occurred. The rich fancies of unbowed youth, the visions of long-perished hopes, the shadows of unborn joys, the gay colourings of the dawn of existence—what ever my memory

WILLIAM LE QUEUX

had treasured up, came before me in review, but lived no longer within my heart.

I recollected that truism of Rochefoucauld's: "Il est difficile de definer l'amour: ce qu'on en peut dire est que, dans l'ame, c'est un passion de regner; dans les esprits, c'est une sympathie; et dans le corps, ce n'est qu'une envie cachee et delicate de posseder ce que l'on aime, apres beaucoup de mysteres." Yes, I loved her with all my heart, with all my soul, but to me I recognised that it was not permitted. My duty, the duty I had promised to fulfil to that dying man whose life-story had been a secret romance, was to act as Mabel's protector, and not to become her lover and thus profit by her wealth. Blair had left his secret to me, in order, no doubt, to place me beyond the necessity of fortune-hunting, and as it had been lost it was my duty to him and to myself to spare no effort to recover it.

With these sentiments firmly established within my heart I entered the *wagon-lit* at Calais, and started on the first stage of my journey across Europe from the Channel to the Mediterranean.

Three days later I was strolling up the Via Tornabuoni, in Florence, that thoroughfare of mediaeval palaces, banks, consulates and chemists' shops that had been so familiar to me each winter, until I had taken to hunting in England in preference to the sunshine of the Lung' Arno and the Cascine. Indeed, some of my early years had been spent in Italy, and I had grown to love it, as every Englishman does. In that bright February morning as I passed up the long, crooked street, filled by the nonchalant Florentines and the wealthy foreigners out for an airing, I passed many men and women of my acquaintance. Doney's and Giacosa's, the favourite lounges of the men, were agog with rich idlers sipping cocktails or that seductive *petit verre* known in the Via Tornabuoni as a *piccolo*, the baskets of the flower-sellers gave a welcome touch of colour to the grim grey of the colossal Palace of the Strozzi, while from the consulates the flags of various nations, most conspicuous of all being that of the ever-popular "Major," reminded me that it was the *festa* of Santa Margherita.

In the old days, when I used to live *en pension* with a couple of Italian artillery officers and a Dutch art-student in the top floor of one of those great old palaces in the Via dei Banchi, the Via Tornabuoni used to be my morning walk, for there one meets everybody, the ladies shopping or going to the libraries, and the men gossiping on the kerb—a habit quickly acquired by every Englishman who takes up his abode in Italy.

It was astonishing, too, what a crowd of well-known faces I passed that morning—English peers and peeresses, Members of Parliament, financial magnates, City sharks, manufacturers, and tourists of every grade and of every nation.

His Highness the Count of Turin, returning from drill, rode by laughing with his aide-de-camp and saluting those he knew. The women mostly wore their smartest toilettes with fur, because a cold wind came up from the Arno, the scent of flowers was in the air, bright laughter and incessant chatter sounded everywhere, and the red-roofed old Lily City was alive with gaiety. Perhaps no city in all the world is so full of charm nor so full of contrasts as quaint old Florence, with her wonderful cathedral, her antique bridge with rows of jewellers' shops upon it, her magnificent churches, her ponderous palaces, and her dark, silent, mediaeval streets, little changed, some of them, since the days when they were trodden by Giotto and by Dante. Time has laid his hand lightly indeed upon the City of Flowers, but whenever he has done so he has altered it out of all recognition, and the garish modernity of certain streets and piazzas surely grates to-day upon those who, like myself, knew the old city before the Piazza Vittorio—always the Piazza Vittorio, synonym of vandalism—had been constructed, and the old Ghetto, picturesque if unclean, was still in existence.

Two men, both of them Italian, stopped to salute me as I walked, and to wish me *ben tomato*. One was an advocate whose wife was accredited one of the prettiest women in that city where, strangely enough, the most striking type of beauty is fair haired. The other was the Cavaliere Alinari, secretary to the British Consul-General, or the "Major," as everybody speaks of him.

I had only arrived in Florence two hours before, and, after a wash at the *Savoy*, had gone forth with the object of cashing a cheque at French's, prior to commencing my inquiries.

Meeting Alinari, however, caused me to halt for a moment, and after he had expressed pleasure at my return, I asked—

"Do you, by any chance, happen to know any one by the name of Melandrini—Paolo Melandrini? His address is given me as Via San Cristofano, number eight."

He looked at me rather strangely with his sharp eyes, stroked his dark beard a moment, and replied in English, with a slight accent—

"The address does not sound very inviting, Mr. Greenwood. I have not the pleasure of knowing the gentleman, but the Via San Cristofano is one of the poorest and worst streets in Florence, just behind Santa Croce from the Via Ghibellina. I should not advise you to enter that quarter at night. There are some very bad characters there."

"Well," I explained, "the fact is I have come down here expressly to ascertain some facts concerning this person."

"Then don't do it yourself," was my friend's strong advice. "Employ some one who is a Florentine. If it is a case of confidential inquiries, he will certainly be much more successful than you can ever be. The moment you set foot in that street it would be known in every tenement that an Inglese was asking questions. And," he added with a meaning smile, "they resent questions being asked in the Via San Cristofano."

VII

The Mysterious Foreigner

I felt that his advice was good, and in further conversation over a *piccolo* at Giacosa's he suggested that I should employ a very shrewd but ugly little old man named Carlini, who sometimes made confidential inquiries on behalf of the Consulate.

An hour later the old man called at the *Savoy*, a bent, shuffling, white-headed old fellow, shabbily dressed, with a grey soft felt rather greasy hat stuck jauntily on the side of his head—a typical Florentine of the people. They called him "Babbo Carlini" in the markets, I afterwards learned, and cooks and servant-girls were fond of playing pranks upon him. Believed by every one to be a little childish, he fostered the idea because it gave him greater facilities in his secret inquiries, for he was regularly employed by the police in serious cases, and through his shrewdness many a criminal had been brought to justice.

In the privacy of my bedroom I explained in Italian the mission I wished him to execute for me.

"Si, signore," was all he responded, and this at every pause I made.

His boots were sadly cracked and down at heel, and he was badly in want of clean linen, but from his handkerchief pocket there arose a small row of "toscani," those long, thin, penny cigars so dear to the Italian palate.

"Recollect," I impressed upon the old fellow, "you must, if possible, find a way of striking up an acquaintance with this individual, Paolo Melandrini, obtain from him all you can about himself, and arrange so that I have, as soon as possible, an opportunity of seeing him without being myself observed. This matter," I added, "is strictly confidential, and I engage you for one week in my service at a wage of two hundred and fifty lire. Here are one hundred to pay your current expenses."

He took the green banknotes in his claw-like hand, and with a muttered "Tanti grazie, signore," transferred it to the inner pocket of his shabby jacket.

"You must on no account allow the man to suspect that any inquiry is being made concerning him. Mind that he knows nothing of any Englishman in Florence asking about him, or it will arouse his suspicions at once. Be very careful in all that you say and do, and report to me tonight. At what time shall I meet you?"

"Late," the old fellow grunted. "He may be a working-man, and if so I shall not be able to see anything of him till evening. I'll call here at eleven o'clock to-night," and then he shuffled out, leaving an odour of stale garlic and strong tobacco.

I began to wonder what the hotel people would think of me entertaining such a visitor, for the *Savoy* is one of the smartest in Florence, but my apprehensions were quickly dispelled, for as we passed out I heard the uniformed hall-porter exclaim in Italian—

"Hulloa, Babbo! Got a fresh job?"

To which the old fellow only grinned in satisfaction, and with another grunt passed out into the sunshine.

That day passed long and anxiously. I idled on the Ponte Vecchio and in the dim religious gloom of the Santissima Anunziata, in the afternoon making several calls upon friends I had known, and in the evening dining at Doney's in preference to the crowded *table-d'hote* of English and Americans at the *Savoy*.

At eleven I awaited old Carlini in the hall of the hotel, and on his arrival took him anxiously in the lift up to my room.

"Well," he commenced, speaking in his slightly-lisping Florentine tongue, "I have been pursuing inquiries all day, but have discovered very little. The individual you require appears to be a mystery."

"I expected so," was my reply. "What have you discovered regarding him?"

"They know him in Via San Cristofano. He has a small apartment on the third floor of number eight, which he only visits occasionally. The place is looked after by an old woman of eighty, whom I managed to question. Discovering that this Melandrini was absent and that a cloth was hanging from the window to dry, I presented myself as an agent of police to explain that the hanging out of a cloth was a contravention of the law and liable to a fine of two francs. I then obtained from her a few facts concerning her *padrone*. She told me all she knew, which did not amount to much. He had a habit of arriving suddenly, generally at evening, and staying there for one or two days, never emerging in the daytime. Where he lived at other times she did not know. Letters often came for him bearing an English stamp, and she kept them. Indeed, she showed me one that arrived ten days ago and is now awaiting him."

Could it be from Blair, I wondered?

"What was the character of the handwriting on the envelope?" I inquired.

"An English hand—thick and heavy. Signore was spelt wrongly, I noticed."

Blair's hand was thick, for he generally wrote with a quill. I longed to examine it for myself.

"Then this old serving-woman has no idea of the individual's address?"

"None whatever. He told her that if any one ever called for him to say that his movements are uncertain, and that any message must be left in writing."

"What is the place like?"

"Poorly furnished, and very dirty and neglected. The old woman is nearly blind and very feeble."

"Does she describe him as a gentleman?"

"I could not ask her for his description, but from inquiries in other quarters I learned that he was in all probability a person who was in trouble with the police, or something of that sort. A man who kept a wine-shop at the end of the street told me in confidence that about six months before, two men, evidently agents of police, had been very active in their inquiries concerning him. They had set a watch upon the house for a month, but he had not returned. He described him as, a middle-aged man with a beard, who was very reticent, who wore glasses, spoke with just a slight foreign accent, and who seldom entered any wine-shop and who scarcely ever passed the time of day with his neighbours. Yet he was evidently well off, for on several occasions, on hearing of distress among the families living in that street, he had surreptitiously visited them and dispensed charity to a no mean degree. Apparently it is this which has inspired respect, while, in addition, he seems to have purposely surrounded his identity by mystery."

"With some object, no doubt," I remarked.

"Certainly," was the queer old man's response. "All my inquiries tend to show he is a man of secrecy and that he is concealing his real identity."

"It may be that he keeps those rooms merely as an address for letters," I suggested.

"Do you know, signore, that is my own opinion?" he said. "He may live in another part of Florence for aught we know."

"We must find out. Before I leave here it is imperative that I should know all about him, therefore I will assist you to watch for his return."

Babbo shook his head and fingered his long cigar, which he was longing to smoke.

"No, signore. You must not appear in the Via San Cristofana. They would note your presence instantly. Leave all to me. I will employ an assistant, and we shall, I hope, before long be shadowing this mysterious individual."

Recollecting that strange letter in Italian which I had secured from the dead man's effects, I asked the old fellow if he knew any place called San Frediano—the place appointed for the meeting between the man now dead and the writer of the letter.

"Certainly," was his reply. "There is the market of San Frediano behind the Carmine. And, of course, there is the Church of San Frediano in Lucca."

"In Lucca!" I echoed. "Ah, but it is not Florence."

Nevertheless, now I recollected, the letter distinctly appointed the hour of meeting "at vespers." The place arranged was therefore most certainly a church.

"Do you know of any other Church of San Frediano?" I inquired.

"Only the one in Lucca."

It was evident, then, that the meeting was to take place there on the 6th of March. If I did not ascertain any further facts concerning Paolo Melandrini in the meantime, I resolved to keep the appointment and watch who should be present.

I gave Carlini permission to smoke, and, seated in a low easy-chair, the old fellow soon filled my room with the strong fumes of his cheap cigar, at the same time relating to me in narrow details all that he had gathered in that Florentine slum.

The secret connexion between Burton Blair and this mysterious Italian was a problem I could not solve. There was evidently some strong motive why he should appoint him controller of Mabel's fortune, yet it was all an utter enigma, just as much as the mysterious source from which the millionaire had obtained his vast wealth.

Whatever we discovered I knew that it must be some strange revelation. From the first moment I had met the wayfarer and his daughter, they had been surrounded by striking romance, which had now deepened, and become more inexplicable by the death of that bluff, hearty man with a secret.

I could not help strongly suspecting that the man Melandrini, whose movements were so mysterious and suspicious, had had some hand in filching from Blair that curious little possession of his which he had, in his will, bequeathed to my keeping. This was a strange fancy of mine, and one which, try how I would, I could not put aside. So erratic seemed the man's movements that, for aught I knew, he might have been in England at the time of Blair's death—if so, then the suspicion against him was gravely increased.

I was feverishly anxious to return to London, but unable yet to do so ere my inquiries were completed. A whole week went by, and Carlini, employing his son-in-law, a dark-haired young man of low class, as his assistant, kept vigilant watch upon the house both night and day, but to no avail. Paolo Melandrini did not appear to claim the letter from England that was awaiting him.

One evening by judiciously bribing the old servant with twenty francs, Carlini obtained the letter in question, and brought it for me to see. In the privacy of my room we boiled a kettle, steamed the flap of the envelope, and took out the sheet of notepaper it contained.

It was from Blair. Dated from Grosvenor Square eighteen days before, it was in English, and read as follows:—

> "*I will meet you if you really wish it. I will bring out the papers with me and trust in you to employ persons who know how to keep their mouths shut. My address in reply will be Mr. John Marshall, Grand Hotel, Birmingham.*
>
> *B.B.*

The mystery increased. Why did Blair wish for the employment of persons who would remain silent? What was the nature of the work that was so very confidential?

Evidently Blair took every precaution in receiving communications from the Italian, causing him to address his letters in various names to various hotels whither he went to stay a night, and thus claim them.

Mabel had often told me of her father's frequent absences from home, he sometimes being away a week or fortnight, or even three weeks, without leaving his address behind. His erratic movements were now accounted for.

Consumed by anxiety I waited day after day, spending hours on that maddening cipher on the playing-card, until, on the morning of the 6th of March, Carlini having been unsuccessful in Florence, I took him

WILLIAM LE QUEUX

with me up to the old city of Lucca, which, travelling by way of Pistoja, we reached about two o'clock in the afternoon.

At the *Universo* I was given that enormous bedroom with the wonderful frescoes which was for so long occupied by Ruskin, and just before the Ave Maria clanged away over the hills and plains, I parted from Babbo and strolled tourist-wise into the magnificent old mediaeval church, the darkness of which was illuminated only by the candles burning at the side altars and the cluster before the statue of Our Lady.

Vespers were in progress, and the deathlike stillness of the great interior was only broken by the low murmuring of the bowed priest.

Only about a dozen persons were present, all of them being women—all save one, a man who, standing back in the shadow behind one of the huge circular columns, was waiting there in patience, while of the others all were kneeling.

Turning suddenly on hearing my light footstep upon the marble flags, I met him next second face to face.

I drew a quick breath, then stood rooted to the spot in blank and utter amazement.

The mystery was far greater than even I had imagined it to be. The truth that dawned upon me was staggering and utterly bewildering.

VIII

In which the Truth is Spoken

The fine old church, with its heavy gildings, its tawdry altars and its magnificent frescoes, was in such gloom that at first, on entering from the street, I could distinguish nothing plainly, but as soon as my eyes became accustomed to the light I saw within a few yards of me a countenance that was distinctly familiar, a face that caused me to pause in anxious breathlessness.

Standing there, behind those scattered kneeling women, with the faint, flickering light of the altar candles illuminating his face just sufficiently, the man's head was bowed in reverence and yet his dark, beady eyes seemed darting everywhere. By his features—those hard, rather sinister features and greyish scraggy beard that I had once before seen—I knew that he was the man who had made the secret appointment with Burton Blair, yet, contrary to my expectations, he was attired in the rough brown habit and rope girdle of a Capuchin lay brother, a silent, mournful figure as he stood with folded arms while the priest in his gorgeous vestments mumbled the prayers.

In that twilight a sepulchral chill fell upon my shoulders; the sweet smell of the incense in the darkness seemed to increase with that world of incredible magnificence, of solitude gloomily enchanted, of wealth strangely incongruous with the squalor and poverty in the piazza outside. Beyond that silent monk whose piercing mysterious eyes were fixed upon me so inquiringly were dark receding distances, traversed here and there by rainbow beams that fell from some great window, while far off a dim red light was suspended from the high, vaulted roof.

Those columns beside which I was standing rose straight to the roof, close and thick like high forest trees, testifying to the patient work of a whole generation of men all carved in living stone, all infinitely durable in spite of such rare delicacy and already transmitted to us from afar through the long-past centuries.

The monk, that man whose bearded face I had seen once before in England, had thrown himself upon his knees, and was mumbling to himself and fingering the huge rosary suspended from his girdle.

A woman dressed in black with the black *santuzza* of the Lucchesi over her head had entered noiselessly, and was prostrated a few feet from me. She held a miserable baby at her breast, a child but a few months old, in whose shrivelled little face there was already the stamp of death. She was praying ardently for him, as the tapers gradually diminished, the penny tapers she had placed before the humble picture of Sant' Antonio, this sorrowing creature. The contrast between the prodigious wealth around and the rags of the humble supplicant was overwhelming and cruel; between the persistent durability of those many thousand Saints draped in gold, and the frailty of that little being with no tomorrow.

The woman was still kneeling, her lips moving in obstinate and vain repetitions. She looked at me, her eyes full of desolation, divining a pity no doubt in mine; then she turned her gaze upon the hooded Capuchin, the hard-faced, bearded man who held the key to the secret of Burton Blair.

I stood behind the ponderous column, bowed but watchful. The poor woman, after a quick glance at the splendour around, turned her eyes more anxiously upon me—a stranger. Did I really think they would listen to her, those magnificent divinities?

Ah! I did not know if they would listen. In her place I would rather have carried the child to one of those wayside shrines where the Virgin of the *contadini* reigns. The Madonnas and Saints of Ghirlandajo and Civitali and Della Querica who inhabited that magnificent old church seemed somehow to be creatures of ceremony, hardened by secular pomp. Strange as it may seem, I could not imagine that they would occupy themselves with a poor old woman from the olive mill or with her deformed and dying child.

Vespers ended. The dark, murmuring figures rose, shuffling away over the marble floor towards the door, and as the lights were quickly extinguished, the woman and her child became swallowed up in the gloom.

I loitered, desiring that the Capuchin should pass me, in order that I could obtain a further view of him. Should I address him, or should I remain silent and set Babbo to watch him?

He approached me slowly, his big hands hidden in the ample sleeves of his snuff-coloured habit, the garment which men of his order have new only once in ten years, and which they wear always, waking or sleeping.

I had halted before the ancient tomb of Santa Zita, that patroness of Lucca whom Dante mentions in his *Inferno*. In the little chapel a single light was burning in the great antique lantern of gold, which the proud Lucchese placed there ages ago when the black plague was feared. As I turned, I saw that, although watching me narrowly, he still seemed to be awaiting the appearance of the man who was now, alas! no more. Yes, now that in a better light I could see his features, I had no hesitation in pronouncing him to be the same man I had met a year ago at Burton's table in Grosvenor Square.

I recollected the occasion well. It was in June, in the height of the London season, and Blair had invited me to dine with several bachelor friends and go to the Empire afterwards. The man now in a religious habit, shuffling along in his worn-out sandals, had presented the very different figure of the easy-going prosperous man-of-the-world, with a fine diamond in his shirt-front and a particularly well-cut dinner jacket. Burton had introduced him to us as Signor Salvi, the celebrated engineer, and he had sat at table opposite me and chatted in excellent English. He struck me as a man who had travelled very widely, especially in the Far East, and from certain expressions he let drop I concluded that, like Burton Blair, he had been to sea, and that he was a friend of the old days before the great secret became so profitable.

The other men present on that occasion were all acquaintances of mine, two of them financiers in the City whose names were well known on the Stock Exchange, a third the heir to an earldom to which he had since succeeded, and the fourth Sir Charles Webb, a smart young Guardsman of the modern type. After a dinner of that exquisite character of which Burton Blair's French *chef* was famous, we all drove to the Empire, and afterwards spent a couple of hours at the Grosvenor Club, concluding the evening at the Bachelors, of which Sir Charles was a member.

Now as I stood within the hushed gloom of that grand old church, watching the dark mysterious figure pacing the aisle in patience and awaiting the person who would never come, I recollected what had, on that evening long ago, aroused within me a curious feeling of resentment against him. It was this. Having left the Empire, we were standing outside on the pavement in Leicester Square calling cabs, when I overheard the Italian exclaim in his own language to Blair, "I do not like that friend of yours—Greenwood. He is far too inquisitive." At this my friend laughed, saying, "Ah, *caro mio*, you don't know him. He is my

WILLIAM LE QUEUX

very best friend." The Italian grunted, replying, "He has been putting leading questions to me all the evening, and I have had to lie to him." Again Blair laughed. "It is not the first time you've committed that sin," was his answer. "No," the other responded in a low voice, intending that I should not overhear him, "but if you introduce me to your friends be careful that they are not quite so astute or so inquisitive as this man Greenwood. He may be a good fellow, but even if he is he surely must not know our secret, if he did, it might mean ruin to us, remember!"

And then, before Blair could make response, he mounted into a hansom which at that moment had pulled up at the kerb.

From that moment I had entertained a distinct dislike of the man who had been introduced to me as Salvi, not that I hold every foreigner in suspicion as some insular Englishmen so foolishly do, but because he had endeavoured to poison Blair's mind against me. Yet after a week the incident had entirely slipped my memory and I had never recollected it until that strange and unexpected re-encounter.

Was it possible that this monk with the sun-bronzed, bearded face was the same man who rented that apartment in the Florence slum, and whose visits there were so surreptitious and mysterious? Perhaps so, because all the secrecy of his habitation would be accounted for by the fact that a Capuchin is not allowed to possess any property outside his monastery. Those infrequent visits to Florence might be made at times when, being a lay brother, he would no doubt be sent out into the country to collect from the *contadini* alms and presents in kind for the poor in the city. Everywhere throughout Tuscany, in peasant's hut as in prince's palace, the humble, patient and charitable Capuchin is welcomed; a flask of wine and a crust is ready for him at the house of every *contadino*, and in the villas and palaces of the rich there is always a place for him in the servants' hall. How many of the Italian poor are saved annually from sheer starvation by the soup and bread dispensed daily at the door of every Capuchin monastery, it would be impossible to estimate. Suffice it to say that the Order in their snuff-coloured habits and their black skull-caps is the greatest and truest friend the starving poor possesses.

Babbo Carlini was no doubt idling outside upon the steps of the church awaiting my reappearance. Would he, I wondered, recognise in this monk the description he had obtained of Paolo Melandrini, the unknown man who was to be Mabel Blair's secretary and adviser?

The last loiterers in the antique Chapel of the Holy Sacrament had left, their footsteps echoing away across the flags to the exit, and I found myself alone with the silent, almost statuesque, man beside whom I had, only one year before stood in the Grand Circle at the Empire watching and criticising a ballet.

Should I address him and claim acquaintance? His openly-expressed disapproval of myself caused me to hesitate. It was quite apparent that he had held me in apprehension on that night at Grosvenor Square, therefore in the present circumstances his suspicion would undoubtedly become increased. Should I boldly address him and thus show my fearlessness, as well as my acquaintance with his subterfuges? or should I withdraw and watch his subsequent movements?

I at length decided on the former course—for two reasons. The first was that I felt confident he had recognised me as Burton's friend; and the second because in dealing with such a man the open declaration of knowledge is always the more advantageous in the end than the careful concealment of such facts as I already knew. If I set a watch upon him his suspicions would become heightened, whereas if I acted openly I might succeed in disarming him.

Therefore, turning upon my heel, I strolled straight towards where he had halted as though he were patiently awaiting Blair's arrival.

"Pardon me, signore," I exclaimed in Italian, "but if I mistake not we have met before—in London, a year ago—was it not?"

"Ah," he exclaimed, his face relaxing into a pleasant smile as he extended his big, hard hand, "I have been wondering all this time, Signor Greenwood, if you would recognise me is this dress. I am very pleased to resume our acquaintance—very." And he emphasised his words, meant or feigned, by a strong, close grip.

I expressed surprise at finding the erratic traveller and man-of-the-world to be, in reality, an inhabitant of the cloister, to which in a low voice, in reverence that we were within that sacred place, he responded—

"I will tell you all about it later. It is not so remarkable as it no doubt strikes you. As a Capuchin I assure you my quiet, reflective life is far preferable to that of the man who, like yourself, mixes with the world and is compelled to live the fevered life of to-day, wherein fortunate unscrupulousness is accounted meritorious and the greatest of sins is that of one's evil living being found out."

"Yes, I quite understand," I replied, surprised nevertheless at his assertion and wondering whether, after all, he was merely attempting to mislead me. "The life of the cloister must be one of a sweet and infinite calm. But if I mistake not," I added, "you are here by appointment to meet our mutual friend, Burton Blair."

He raised his dark eyebrows slightly, and I could have sworn that my words caused him to start. Yet so cleverly did he conceal any surprise I had caused him that he replied in a quiet, natural tone—

"That is so. I am here to see him."

"Then I regret to tell you that you will never see him again," I said in a low, earnest voice.

"Why?" he gasped, his black eyes wide open in surprise.

"Because," I answered, "because poor Burton Blair is dead—and his secret has been stolen."

"What!" he cried, with a look of abject terror and in a voice so loud that his exclamation echoed along the high, vaulted roof. "Blair dead—and the secret stolen! *Dio*! impossible—impossible!"

IX

The House of Silence

The effect of my words upon the burly Capuchin, whose form seemed almost gigantic on account of the thickness of his inartistic habit, was as curious as it was unexpected.

My announcement of Blair's death seemed to completely unnerve him. Apparently he had been waiting there, keeping the appointment, all unconscious of the untimely end of the man with whom he had been on terms of such secret and intimate friendship.

"Tell me—tell me how it happened," he gasped in Italian in a low, hushed voice, as though he feared that some eavesdropper might be lurking in those dark recesses.

In a few brief words I explained the truth, to which he listened in silence. Then, when I had finished, he muttered something, crossed himself, and, as the approaching footsteps of the sacristan aroused us both, we walked forward and out into the dusk of the broad piazza.

Old Carlini, was was lounging upon a bench smoking the end of a cigar, noticed us in an instant and I saw him open his eyes in wonderment, although further than that he betrayed no sign.

"Poverino! Poverino!" repeated the monk as we strolled together slowly beside the old red walls of the once-proud city. "To think that our poor friend Burton died so suddenly—and without a word!"

"Not exactly without a word," I said. "He gave several directions, one of which was that he placed his daughter Mabel beneath my care."

"Ah, the little Mabel," he sighed. "Surely it is ten years since I saw her in Manchester. She was then about eleven, a tall, dark-haired, rather pretty child, a striking likeness of her mother—poor woman."

"You knew her mother, then?" I asked in some surprise.

He nodded in the affirmative, but gave no further information.

Suddenly turning to me as we walked towards the city gate, the Ponto Santa Maria, where the uniformed officers of the *dazio* were lounging ready to tax every pennyworth of food-stuff entering there, he demanded—

"How did you know that I had an appointment with our friend to-night?"

"By the letter which you wrote him, and which was found in his bag after his decease," I responded frankly.

He grunted with distinct satisfaction. It struck me indeed as though he were apprehensive that Burton had before his death told me some details regarding his life. I recollected that curious cipher upon the playing-card, although I made no reference to it.

"Ah! I see!" he exclaimed presently. "But if that little wallet, or whatever it was, that he always wore either concealed within his clothes or suspended around his neck, is missing, does not it point to a tragedy—theft and murder?"

"There are distinct suspicions," was my reply. "Although, according to the doctors, he died from a purely natural cause."

"Ah! I don't believe it!" cried the monk, fiercely clenching his fist. "One of them has succeeded at last in stealing that sachet of which he was always so very careful, and I'm positive that murder has been committed in order to conceal the theft."

"One of whom?" I inquired anxiously.

"One of his enemies."

"But are you aware what that little bag contained?"

"He never would tell me," was the Capuchin's reply, looking me straight in the face. "He only said that his secret was concealed within—and I have reason to believe that such was a fact."

"But you knew his secret?" I said, my eyes full upon him.

I noted, by the change in his dark countenance, how my allegation caused him quick apprehension. He could not totally deny it, yet he was certainly seeking some means of misleading me.

"I only know what he explained to me," he responded. "And that was not much, for, as you are aware, he was a most reticent man. He has long ago related to me, however, the somewhat romantic circumstances in which you met, what a good friend you were to him before his stroke of fortune, and how you and your friend—I forget his name—put Mabel to school at Bournemouth, and thus rescued her from that weary tramp which Burton himself had undertaken."

"But why was he on tramp in that manner?" I asked. "To me it has always been an enigma."

"And also to me. He was, I believe, in search of the key to that secret which he carried with him—the secret which, you say, he has bequeathed to you."

"Did he reveal to you nothing more?" I inquired, recollecting that from this man's remarks regarding Mabel's youth, he and Blair must have been old friends.

"Nothing. His secret remained his own, and he revealed it to nobody always fearing betrayal."

"But now that it is in other hands, what do you anticipate?" I inquired, still walking at his side, for we had passed out of the city and were out upon that wide, dirty road that led away to the Moriano Bridge and then fifteen miles up into the mountains to that leafy and rather gay summer resort well known to all Italians and some English, the Baths of Lucca.

"Well," responded my companion, very gravely, "from what I learned in London on the occasion we met, I anticipate that poor Blair's secret has been most ingeniously stolen, and will be put to good account by the person into whose possession it has now passed."

"To the detriment of his daughter Mabel?"

"Most certainly. She must be the principal sufferer," he replied, with just a suspicion of a sigh.

"Ah, if he had only confided his affairs in some one who, knowing the truth, might have combated this cunning conspiracy! But, as it is, we seem all utterly in the dark. Even his lawyers know nothing!"

"And you, to whom the secret is left, have actually lost it!" he added. "Yes, signore, the situation is indeed a most critical one."

"In this affair, Signor Salvi," I said, "being mutual friends of poor Blair, we must endeavour to do our best to discover and punish his enemies. Tell me, therefore, if you are aware of the source of our unfortunate friend's vast wealth?"

"I am not Signor Salvi here," was the monk's quiet reply. "I am known as Fra Antonio of Arezzo, or Fra Antonio for short. The name of Salvi was given to me by poor Blair himself, who did not wish to introduce a Capuchin among his worldly friends as such. As to the source of his wealth, I believe I am acquainted with the truth."

"Then tell me, tell me!" I cried anxiously.

"For it may give us the clue to these persons who had so successfully conspired against him." Again the monk turned his dark, penetrating eyes upon me, those eyes that in the gloom of San Frediano had seemed so full of fire and yet so full of mystery.

"No," he answered in a hard, decisive tone. "I am not permitted to tell anything. He is dead—let his memory rest."

WILLIAM LE QUEUX

"But why?" I demanded. "In these circumstances of grave suspicion, and of the theft of the secret which is my property by right, it is surely your duty to explain what you know, in order that we may gain a clue? Recollect, too, that the future of his daughter depends upon the truth being revealed."

"I can tell you nothing," he repeated. "Much as I regret it, my lips are sealed."

"Why?"

"By an oath taken years ago—before I entered the Order of the Capuchins," he responded. Then after a pause, he added, with a sigh, "It is all strange—stranger perhaps than any man has dreamed—yet I can tell you nothing, Mr. Greenwood, absolutely nothing."

I was silent. His words were highly tantalising, as well as disappointing. I had not yet made up my mind whether he was actually my enemy or my friend.

At one moment he seemed simple, honest and straightforward as are all men of his religious order, yet at others there seemed within him that craft and cunning, that clever diplomacy and far-seeing acumen of the Jesuit, traits of a character warped into ingenuity and double-dealing.

The very fact that Burton Blair had always hidden from me his friendship—if friendship it were—for this stalwart monk with the bronzed and furrowed face, caused me to entertain a kind of vague distrust in him. And yet, when I recollected the tone of the letter he had written to Blair, how could I doubt but their friendship, if secret, was a real and genuine one? Nevertheless, I recollected those words I had overheard on the pavement of Leicester Square, and they caused me to ponder and to doubt.

I walked on beside this man, heedless of our destination. We were quite in the country now. The immobility of everything, the luminous brilliancy of the tints of that winter afterglow gave the grey, olive-clad Tuscan hills something of sadness. That great, calm silence over everything, that unchanging stillness in the air, those motionless lights and great shadows gave one the impression of a pause in the dizzy movement of centuries, of a reflectiveness, of an intense waiting, or rather a look of melancholy thrown back on a past anterior to suns and human beings, races and religions.

Before us, as we rounded a bend in the road, I saw a huge, white old monastery standing high upon the hillside half hidden by the grey-green trees.

It was the Convent of the Cappuccini, he told me—his home.

I halted for a moment, gazing upon the white, almost windowless building, scorched by three hundred summers, standing like a stronghold, as once it was, against the background of the purple Apennines. I listened to the clanking of the old bell that sent out its summons with the same note of age, the same old voice as in centuries gone. It was then, in that moment, that the charm of old-world Lucca and her beautiful surroundings became impressed upon me. I felt, for the first time, stealing up from everywhere, an atmosphere of separateness, as it were, from the rest of the world, of mystery—a living essence of what the place is—destructible, alas! but still impregnating all things, exhaling from all things—surely the dying soul of once-brilliant Tuscany.

And there beside me, overwhelming all my thoughts, as the shadow of the giant Sphinx falls lengthening upon the desert sands, stood that big, bronzed monk in the faded brown habit, his feet bare, his waist bound by a hempen cord, his countenance a mystery, yet within his heart the great secret which no power could induce him to divulge—the secret of wealth that had been bequeathed to me.

"Poor Blair is dead!" he repeated again and again in fairly good English, as though almost unable as yet to realise that his friend was no more. Nevertheless, I was slow to become convinced that he spoke seriously. He might be misleading me, after all.

At his invitation I accompanied him up the steep, winding road until we came to the ponderous gate of the monastery, at which he rang. A solemn bell clanged loudly, and a few moments later the little grille was opened, revealing the white-bearded face of the janitor, who instantly admitted us.

He took me across the silent cloister, in the middle of which was a wonderful mediaeval well of wrought ironwork, and then along endless stone corridors, each lit by its single oil lamp, which rendered the place only more gloomy and depressing.

From the chapel at the end of the great building came the low chanting of the monks, but beyond, the quiet was that of the grave. The dark, ghostly figures passed us noiselessly and seemed to draw aside into the darkness; the door of the refectory stood open, showing by the two or three dim lights magnificent carvings, wonderful frescoes and the two long rows of time-blackened oak benches at which the Brothers sat at meals.

Suddenly my conductor stopped before a small door, which he

WILLIAM LE QUEUX

opened with his key, and I found myself within a tiny, carpetless cubicle containing a truckle bed, a chair, a well-filled bookcase and a writing-table. Upon the wall was a large wooden crucifix before which he crossed himself on entering.

"This is my home," he explained in English. "Not very luxurious, it is true, but I would not exchange it for a palace in the world outside. Here we are all brothers, with the superior as our father to supply us with all our worldly wants, even to our snuff. There are no jealousies, no bickerings, no backbitings or rivalry. All are equal, all perfectly contented, for we have each one of us learnt the very difficult lesson of brotherly love." And he drew the single chair for me to seat myself, for I was hot and tired after that long, steep ascent from the town.

"It is surely a hard life," I observed.

"At first, yes. One must be strong in body and in mind to successfully pass the period of probation," he answered. "But afterwards the Capuchin's life is surely one of the pleasantest on earth, banded as we are to do good and to exercise charity in the name of Sant' Antonio. But," he added, with a smile, "I did not bring you here, signore, to endeavour to convert you from your Protestant faith. I asked you to accompany me, because you have told me what is a profound and remarkable mystery. You have told me of the death of Burton Blair, the man who was my friend, and to whose advantage it was to meet me in San Frediano to-night. There were reasons—the very strongest reasons a man could have—why he should have kept the appointment. But he has not done so. His enemies have willed it otherwise, and they have stolen his secret!" While he spoke he fumbled in a drawer of the little deal writing-table, and drew forth something, adding in deep earnestness—

"You knew poor Blair intimately—more intimately, perhaps, than I did of later years. You knew his enemies as well as his friends. Tell me, have you ever met the original of either of these men?"

And he held before my gaze two cabinet photographs.

One of them was quite unfamiliar to me, but the other I recognised in an instant.

"Why!" I said, "that's my old friend Reginald Seton—Blair's friend."

"No," the monk declared in a hard, meaning tone, "not his friend, signore—his bitterest enemy."

X

The Man of Secrets

I don't understand you," I exclaimed, resenting this charge against the man who was my most intimate friend. "Seton has been even a better friend to poor Blair than myself."

Fra Antonio smiled strangely and mysteriously, as only the subtle Italian can. He seemed to pity my ignorance, and inclined to humour me in my belief in Seton's genuineness.

"I know," he laughed. "I know almost as much as you do upon the one side, while upon the other my knowledge extends somewhat further. All I can say is that I have watched, and have formed my own conclusions."

"That Seton was not his friend?"

"That Seton was not his friend," he repeated slowly and very distinctly.

"But surely you make no direct charge against him?" I cried. "You surely don't think he's responsible for this tragedy—if tragedy it really is."

"I make no direct charge," was his ambiguous reply. "Time will reveal the truth—no doubt."

I longed to ask him straight out whether he did not sometimes go under the name of Paolo Melandrini, yet I feared to do so lest I should arouse his suspicion unduly.

"Time can only reveal that Reginald Seton has been one of the dead man's best friends," I said reflectively.

"Outwardly, yes," was the Capuchin's dubious remark.

"An enemy as deadly as the Ceco?" I inquired, watching his face the while.

"The Ceco!" he gasped, instantly taken aback by my bold remark. "Who told you of him? What do you know regarding him?"

The monk had evidently forgotten what he had written in that letter to Blair.

"I know that he is in London," I responded, taking my cue from his own words. "The girl is with him," I added, utterly unaware however of the identity of the person referred to.

"Well?" he asked.

"And if they are in London it is surely for no good purpose?"

"Ah!" he said. "Blair has told you something—told you of his suspicions?"

"Of late he has gone about in daily dread of secret assassination," I replied. "He was evidently afraid of the Ceco."

"And surely he had need to be," exclaimed Fra Antonio, his dark, brilliant eyes again turned upon mine in the semi-darkness. "The Ceco is not an individual to be dealt with easily."

"But what took him to London?" I demanded. "Did he go with harmful intentions?"

The burly monk shrugged his shoulders, answering—

"Dick Dawson was never of a very benevolent disposition. He evidently discovered something, and swore to be avenged."

His remarks made plain one very important fact, namely, that the man who went by the nickname of the "blind man" in Italy was really an Englishman of the name of Dick Dawson—an adventurer most probably.

"Then you suspect him of complicity in the theft of the secret?" I suggested.

"Well, as the little sachet of chamois leather is missing, I am inclined to think that it must have passed into his hands."

"And the girl, what of her?"

"His daughter, Dolly, will assist him, that's plain. She's as shrewd as her father, and possesses a woman's cunning into the bargain—a dangerous girl, to say the least. I warned poor Blair of them both," he added, suddenly, it seemed, recollecting his letter. "But I am glad you have recognised one of these photographs. His name is Seton, you say. Well, if he is your friend, take my advice and beware. Are you certain you have never seen this other man—a friend of Seton's?" he asked very earnestly.

I carried the picture in my hand to where the dim oil lamp was burning, and examined it very closely. It was a vignette of a long-faced, bald-headed, full-bearded man, wearing a stand-up collar, a black frock-coat and well-tied bow cravat. The stud in his shirt front was somewhat peculiar, for it seemed like the miniature cross of some foreign order of chivalry, and produced a rather neat and novel effect. The eyes were those of a keen, crafty man, and the hollow cheeks gave the countenance a slightly haggard and striking appearance.

It was a face that, to my recollection, I had never seen before, yet such were its peculiarities that they at once became photographed indelibly upon my memory.

I told him of my failure to recognise who it was, whereupon he urged—

"When you return, watch the movements of your so-called friend Seton, and you will perhaps meet his friend. When you do, write to me here, and leave him to me." And he replaced the photograph in the drawer, but as he did so my quick eye detected that within was a playing card, the seven of clubs, with some letters written upon it very similar to those upon the card in my pocket. I mentioned it, but he merely smiled and quickly closed the drawer.

Yet surely the fact of the cipher being in his possession was more than strange.

"Do you ever travel away from Lucca?" I inquired at last, recollecting how I had met him at Blair's table in Grosvenor Square, but not at all satisfied regarding the discovery of the inscribed card.

"Seldom—very seldom," he answered. "It is so difficult to obtain permission, and then it is only given to visit relatives. If there is any monastery in the vicinity of our destination we must beg our bed there, in preference to remaining in a private house. The rules sound irksome to you," he added with a smile. "But I assure you they do not gall us in the least. They are beneficial to man's happiness and comfort, all of them."

Again I turned the conversation, endeavouring to ascertain some facts concerning the dead man's mysterious secret, which I somehow felt convinced was known to him. But all to no avail. He would tell me nothing.

All he explained was that the reason of the appointment in Lucca that evening was a very strong one, and that if alive the millionaire would undoubtedly have kept it.

"He was in the habit of meeting me at certain intervals either in the Church of San Frediano, or at other places in Lucca, in Pescia, or Pistoja," the monk said. "We generally varied the place of meeting from time to time."

"And that, of course, accounts for his mysterious absences from home," I remarked, for his movements were frequently very erratic, so that even Mabel was unaware of his address. He was generally supposed, however, to be in the North of England or in Scotland. No one had any idea that he travelled so far afield as Central Italy.

The monk's statement also made it plain that Blair had some very strong motive for keeping these frequent appointments. Fra Antonio, his secret friend, had undoubtedly also been his most intimate and most trusted one.

Why had he kept this strange and mysterious friendship from us all—even from Mabel?

I gazed upon the Italian's hard, sunburnt face and tried to penetrate the mystery written there, but in vain. No man can keep a secret like the priest of the confessional, or the monk in his cell.

"And what is your intention, now that poor Blair is dead?" I asked at length.

"My intention, like yours, is to discover the truth," he replied. "It will be a difficult matter, no doubt, but I trust that we shall, in the end, succeed, and that you will regain the lost secret."

"But may not Blair's enemies make use of it in the meantime?" I queried.

"Ah! of course we cannot prevent that," answered Fra Antonio. "We have to look to the future, and allow the present to take care of itself. You, in London, will do your best to discover whether Blair has met with foul play and at whose hands, while I, here in Italy, will try to find out whether there was any further motive than the theft of the secret."

"But if the little chamois-bag had been stolen, would not Blair himself have missed it?" I suggested. "He was quite conscious for several hours before he died."

"He might have forgotten it. Men's memories often fail them completely in the hours preceding death."

Night had fallen before the great wooden clappers, used to arouse the monks to go to prayers at two o'clock in the morning, resounded through the cloister as a reminder that I, a stranger, must take my departure.

Fra Antonio rose, lit a great old brass lantern, and conducted me along those silent corridors, out across the small piazza and down the hillside to the main road which lay straight and white in the darkness.

Then, having directed me on the road, he grasped my hand in his big palm, rough through hard toil at his patch of garden, and said—

"Rely upon me to do my best. I knew poor Blair—yes, knew him better than you did, Signor Greenwood. I knew, too, something of his remarkable secret, and therefore I am aware how strange and how mysterious are all the circumstances. I shall work on here, making inquiries, while you return to London and pursue yours. I would, however, make the suggestion to you that if you meet Dick Dawson strike up a friendship with him, and with Dolly. They are a strange pair, but friendship with them may be profitable."

"What!" I exclaimed. "Friendship with the man whom you declare was one of Blair's bitterest enemies?"

"And why not? Is it not diplomacy to be well received in the enemy's camp? Recollect that your own stake in this affair is the greatest of any one's. The secret is bequeathed to you—the secret of Burton Blair's millions!"

"And I intend to recover it," I declared firmly.

"I only hope you will, signore," he said in a voice which to me sounded full of a double meaning. "I only hope you will."

Then wishing me *Addio, e buona fortuna*," Fra Antonio, the Capuchin and man of secrets, turned and left me standing in the dark highway.

Hardly had I advanced fifty yards before a short dark figure loomed out from the shadow of some bushes, and by the voice that hailed me I knew it to be old Babbo, whom I had believed had grown tired of awaiting me. He had, however, evidently followed us from the church, and seeing us enter the monastery had patiently awaited my return.

"Has the signore discovered what he wished?" inquired the old Italian, quickly.

"Some of it, not all," was my rejoinder. "You saw that monk whom I met?"

"Yes. Since you have been in the convent I have made some inquiries, and find that the most popular Capuchin in the whole of Lucca is Fra Antonio, and that his charitableness is well known. It is he who begs from door to door through the city for contesimi and lire in order that the poor shall have their daily soup and bread. Report accredits him with great wealth, which on entering the Order of the Capuchins he made over as a gift to the fraternity. He is also known to have a friend to whom he is very much attached—an Englishman who has one eye so badly injured that he is known by the townspeople as the Ceco."

"The Ceco!" I cried. "What have you discovered regarding him?"

"The keeper of a little cheese-shop close to the gate by which we left the city proved very communicative. Like all her class, she seemed to greatly admire our friend the Cappuccino. She told me of the frequent visits of this one-eyed Englishman who had lived so long in Italy that he was almost an Italian. The Ceco was in the habit, it seemed, of

WILLIAM LE QUEUX

staying at the old albergo, the *Croce di Malto*, sometimes accompanied by a young and very pretty lady, his daughter."

"Where do they come from?"

"Oh! I've not yet been able to discover that," was Babbo's reply. "It seems, however, that the constant visits of the Ceco to the monastery have aroused the public interest. The people say that Fra Antonio nowadays is not so active in his searches after money for the poor now he is too much occupied with his English friend."

"And the girl?"

"It is evident that her beauty is remarkable, even in Lucca, this city of pretty girls," answered the old man with a grin. "She speaks Tuscan perfectly, and could, they say, easily pass for an Italian. Her back is not straight like those Inglese one sees in the Via Tornabuoni—if the signore will pardon the criticism," the old fellow added apologetically.

This proof that Dick Dawson, against whom the monk had warned Burton Blair, was actually the friend of the Capuchin brother rendered the situation more puzzling and more complicated. I recognised in these frequent consultations a secret plot against my friend, a conspiracy which had apparently been carried to a successful issue.

The girl Dolly, whoever she was, had of course never been to the monastery, but she had evidently been in Lucca as a participator in the plot to obtain Burton Blair's valuable secret, the secret that was now mine by law.

We there and then resolved to make inquiries at the *Croce di Malto*, that antique old hostelry in a narrow side street peculiarly Italian, and which still prefers to be designated as an albergo, in preference to the modern name of hotel.

Dick Dawson, known as the Ceco, was undoubtedly in London, but with the connivance and aid of that crafty and ingenious man of secrets, who had so cleverly endeavoured to establish with me a false friendship.

Was it actually this man who hid his evil deeds beneath his shabby religious habit who was responsible for the death of poor Blair and the mysterious disappearance of that strange little object which was his most treasured possession. I somehow felt convinced that such was the actual truth.

XI

Which Explains the Peril
of Mabel Blair

From inquiries made by old Babbo next morning at the *Cross of Malta*, it appeared quite plain that Mr. Richard Dawson, whoever he was, constantly visited Lucca, and always with the object of consulting the popular Capuchin brother.

Sometimes the one-eyed Englishman who spoke Italian so well would journey up to the monastery and remain there several hours, and at others Fra Antonio would come to the inn and there remain closeted in closest secrecy with the visitor.

The Ceco, so called because of his defective vision, was apparently a man of means, for his tips to the waiters and maids were always generous, and when a guest, he and his daughter always ordered the best that could be procured. They came from Florence, the *padrone* thought, but of that he was not quite certain. The letters and telegrams he received securing rooms were dispatched from various towns in both France and Italy, which seemed to show that they were constantly travelling.

That was all the information we could gather. The identity of the mysterious Paolo Melandrini was, as yet, unproven. My primary object in travelling to Italy was not accomplished, but I nevertheless felt satisfied that I had at last discovered two of poor Blair's most intimate and yet secret friends.

But why the secrecy? When I recollected how close had been our friendship, I felt surprised, and even a trifle annoyed that he had concealed the existence of these men from me. Much as I regretted to think ill of a friend who was dead, I could not suppress a suspicion that his acquaintance with those men was part of his secret, and that the latter was some dishonourable one.

Soon after midday, I crammed my things into my valise, and, impelled by a strong desire to return to safeguard, the interests of Mabel Blair, left Lucca for London. Babbo travelled with me as far as Pisa, where we changed, he journeying back to Florence and I picking up the sleeping-car express on its way through from Rome to Calais.

While standing on the platform at Pisa, however, the shabby old man, who had grown, thoughtful during the past half-hour or so, suddenly said—

"A strange idea has occurred to me, ignore. You will recollect that I learned in the Via Cristofano that the Signor Melandrini wore gold-rimmed glasses. Is it possible that he does so in Florence in order to conceal his defective sight?"

"Why—I believe so!" I cried. "I believe you've guessed the truth! But on the other hand, neither his servant nor the neighbours suspected him of being a foreigner."

"He speaks Italian very well," agreed the old man, "but they said he had a slight accent."

"Well," I said, excited at this latest theory. "Return at once to the Via San Cristofano and make further inquiries regarding the mysterious individual's eyesight and his glasses. The old woman who keeps his rooms has no doubt seen him without his glasses, and can tell you the truth."

"Signore," was the old fellow's answer. And I then wrote down for him my address in London to which he was to dispatch a telegram if his suspicions were confirmed.

Ten minutes later, the roaring Calais-Rome express, the limited train of three *wagon-lits*, dining-car and baggage-car, ran into the great vaulted station, and, wishing the queer old Babbo farewell, I climbed in and was allotted my berth for Calais.

To describe the long, wearying journey back from the Mediterranean to the Channel, with those wheels grinding for ever beneath, and the monotony only broken by the announcement that a meal was ready, is useless. You, who read this curious story of a man's secret, who have travelled backwards and forwards over that steel road to Rome, know well how wearisome it becomes, if you have been a constant traveller between England and Italy.

Suffice it to say that thirty-six hours after entering the express at Pisa, I crossed the platform at Charing Cross, jumped into a hansom and drove to Great Russell Street. Reggie was not yet back from his warehouse, but on my table among a quantity of letters I found a telegram in Italian from Babbo. It ran:—

"Melandrini has left eye injured. Undoubtedly same man.

Carlini

The individual who was destined to be Mabel Blair's secretary and adviser was her dead father's bitterest enemy—the Englishman, Dick Dawson.

I stood staring at the telegram, utterly stupefied.

The strange couplet which the dead man had written in his will, and urged upon me to recollect, kept running in my head—

"King Henry the Eighth was a knave to his queens. He'd one short of seven—and nine or ten scenes!"

What hidden meaning could it convey? The historic facts of King Henry's marriages and divorces were known to me just as they were known to every fourth-standard English child throughout the country. Yet there was certainly some motive why Blair should have placed the rhyme there—perhaps as a key to something, but to what?

After a hurried wash and brush up, for I was very dirty and fatigued after my long journey, I took a cab to Grosvenor Square, where I found Mabel dressed in her neat black, sitting alone reading in her own warm, cosy room, an apartment which her father had, two years ago, fitted tastefully and luxuriously as her boudoir.

She sprang to her feet quickly and greeted me in eagerness when the man announced me.

"Then you are back again, Mr. Greenwood," she cried. "Oh, I'm so very glad. I've been wondering and wondering that I had heard no news of you. Where have you been?"

"In Italy," I answered, throwing off my overcoat at her suggestion, and taking a low chair near her. "I have been making inquiries."

"And what have you discovered?"

"Several facts which tend rather to increase the mystery surrounding your poor father than to elucidate it."

I saw that her face was paler than it had been when I left London, and that she seemed unnerved and strangely anxious. I asked her why she had not gone to Brighton or to some other place on the south coast as I had suggested, but she replied that she preferred to remain at home, and that in truth she had been anxiously awaiting my return.

I explained to her in brief what I had discovered in Italy: of my meeting with the Capuchin brother and of our curious conversation.

"I never heard my father speak of him," she said. "What kind of man is he?"

I described him as best I could, and told her how I had met him at dinner there, in their house, during her absence with Mrs. Percival in Scotland.

"I thought that a monk, having once entered an Order, could not re-assume the ordinary garments of secular life," she remarked.

"Neither can he," I said. "That very fact increases the suspicion against him, combined with the words I overheard later outside the Empire Theatre." And then I went on to relate the incident, just as I have written it down in a foregoing chapter.

She was silent for some time, her delicate pointed chin resting upon her palm, as she gazed thoughtfully into the fire. Then at last she asked—

"And what have you found out regarding this mysterious Italian in whose hands my father has left me? Have you seen him?"

"No, I have not seen him, Mabel," was my response. "But I have discovered that he is a middle-aged Englishman, and not an Italian at all. I shall not, I think, be jealous of his attentions to you, for he has a defect—he has only one eye."

"Only one eye!" she gasped, her face blanching in an instant as she sprang to her feet. "A man with one eye—and an Englishman! Why," she cried, "you surely don't say that the man in question is named Dawson—Dick Dawson?"

"Paolo Melandrini and Dick Dawson are one and the same," I said plainly, utterly amazed at the terrifying effect my words had had upon her.

"But surely my father has not left me in the hands of that fiend—the man whose very name is synonymous of all that is cunning, evil and brutal? It can't be true—there must be some mistake, Mr. Greenwood—there must be! Ah! you do not know the reputation of that one-eyed Englishman as I do, or you would wish me dead rather than see me in association with him. You must save me!" she cried in terror, bursting into a torrent of tears. "You promised to be my friend. You must save me, save me from that man—the man whose very touch deals death!" And next instant she reeled, stretched forth her thin white hands wildly, and would have fallen senseless to the floor had I not sprang forward and caught her in my arms.

Whom, I wondered, was this man Dick Dawson that she held in such terror and loathing—this one-eyed man who was evidently a link with her father's mysterious past?

XII

MR. RICHARD DAWSON

I confess that I was longing for the appearance of this one-eyed Englishman of whom Mabel Blair was evidently so terrified, in order to judge him for myself.

What I had gathered concerning him was, up to the present, by no means satisfactory. That, in common with the monk, he held the secret of the dead man's past seemed practically certain, and perhaps Mabel feared some unwelcome revelation concerning her father's actions and the source of his wealth. This was the thought which occurred to me when, having raised the alarm which brought the faithful companion, Mrs. Percival, I was assisting to apply restoratives to the insensible girl.

As she lay, her head pillowed upon a cushion of daffodil silk, Mrs. Percival knelt beside her, and, being in ignorance, held me, I think, in considerable suspicion. She inquired rather sharply the reason of Mabel's unconsciousness, but I merely replied that she had been seized with a sudden faintness, and attributed it to the overheating of the room.

Presently, when she came to, she asked Mrs. Percival and her maid Bowers to leave us alone, and after the door had shut she inquired, pale-faced and anxious—

"When is this man Dawson to come here?"

"When Mr. Leighton gives him notice of the clause in your father's will."

"He can come here," she said determinedly, "but before he crosses this threshold, I shall leave the house. He may act just as he thinks proper, but I will not reside under the same roof with him, nor will I have any communication with him whatsoever."

"I quite understand your feelings, Mabel," I said. "But is such a course a judicious one? Will it not be best to wait and watch the fellow's movements?"

"Ah! but you don't know him!" she cried. "You don't suspect what I know to be the truth!"

"What's that?"

"No," she said in a low hoarse voice, "I may not tell you. You will discover all ere long, and then you will not be surprised that I abhor the very name of the man."

"But why on earth did your father insert such a clause in his will?"

"Because he was compelled," she answered hoarsely. "He could not help himself."

"And if he had refused—refused to place you in the power of such a person—what then?"

"It would have meant his ruin," she answered. "I suspected it all the instant I heard that a mysterious man was to be my secretary and to have control of my affairs. Your discovery in Italy has only confirmed my suspicions."

"But you will take my advice, Mabel, and bear with him at first," I urged, wondering within my heart whether her hatred of the man was because she knew that he was her father's assassin. She entertained some violent dislike of him, but for what reason I entirely failed to discover.

She shook her head at my argument, saying—"I regret that I am not sufficiently diplomatic to be able to conceal my antipathy in that manner. We women are clever in many ways, but we must always exhibit our dislikes," she added.

"Well," I remarked, "it will be a very great pity to treat him with open hostility, for it may upset all our future chances of success in discovering the truth regarding your poor father's death, and the theft of his secret. My strong advice is to remain quite silent, apathetic even, and yet with a keen, watchful eye. Sooner or later this man, if he really is your enemy, must betray himself. Then will be time enough for us to act firmly, and, in the end, you will triumph. For my own part I consider that the sooner Leighton gives the fellow notice of his appointment the better."

"But is there no way by which this can be avoided?" she cried, dismayed. "Surely my poor father's death is sufficiently painful without this second misfortune!"

She spoke to me as frankly as she would have done to a brother, and I recognised by her intense manner how, now that her suspicions were confirmed, she had become absolutely desperate. Amid all the luxury and splendour of that splendid place she was a wan and lonely figure, her young heart torn by grief at her father's death and by a terror which she dare not divulge.

There is an old and oft-repeated saying that wealth does not bring happiness, and surely there is often a greater peace of mind and pure enjoyment of life in the cottage than in the mansion. The poor are apt to regard the rich with envy, yet it should be remembered that many a man and many a woman lolling in a luxurious carriage and served by liveried servants looks forth upon those toilers in the streets, well knowing that the hurrying millions of what they term "the masses" are really far happier than they. Many a disappointed, world-weary woman of title, often young and beautiful, would to-day gladly exchange places with the daughter of the people, whose life, if hard, is nevertheless full of harmless pleasures and as much happiness as can to obtained in this our workaday world. This allegation may sound strange, but I nevertheless declare it to be true. The possession of money may bring luxury and renown; it may enable men and women to outshine their fellows; it may bring honour, esteem and even popularity. But what are they all? Ask the great landowner; ask the wealthy peer; ask the millionaire. If they speak the truth they will tell you in confidence that they are not in their hearts half so happy, nor do they enjoy life so much, as the small man of independent means, the man who is subject to an abatement upon his income-tax.

As I sat there with the dead man's daughter, endeavouring to induce her to receive the mysterious individual without open hostility, I could not help noticing the vivid contrast between the luxury of her surroundings and the heavy burden of her heart.

She suggested that the house should be sold and that she should retire to Mayvill and there live quietly in the country with Mrs. Percival, but I urged her to wait, at least for the present. It seemed a pity that Burton Blair's splendid collection of old masters, and the fine tapestries that he had bought in Spain only a few years ago, and the unique collection of early Majolica, should go to the hammer. Among the many treasures in the dining-room was Andrea del Sarto's "Holy Family," for which Blair had given sixteen thousand five hundred pounds at Christie's, and which was considered one of the finest examples of that great master. Again, the Italian Renaissance furniture, the old Montelupo and Savona ware and the magnificent old English plate were each worth a fortune in themselves, and should, I contended, remain Mabel's property, as they had been all bequeathed to her.

"Yes, I know," she responded to my argument. "Everything is mine except that little bag containing the sachet, which is yours, and which is so unfortunately missing."

"You must help me to recover it," I urged. "It will be to our mutual interests to do so."

"Of course I will assist you in every way possible, Mr. Greenwood," was her answer. "Since you've been away in Italy I have had the house searched from top to bottom, and have myself examined all my father's dispatch-boxes, his two other safes, and certain places where he sometimes secreted his private papers, in order to discover whether, fearing that an attempt might be made to steal the little bag, he left it at home. But all in vain. It certainly is not in this house."

I thanked her for her efforts, knowing well that she had acted vigorously on my behalf, but feeling that any search within that house was futile, and that if the secret were ever recovered it would be found in the hands of one or other of Blair s enemies.

Together we sat for a long time discussing the situation. The reason of her hatred of the man Dawson she would not divulge, but this did not cause me any real surprise, for I saw in her attitude a desire to conceal some secret of her father's past. Nevertheless, after much persuasion, I induced her to consent to allow the man to be informed of his office, and to receive him without betraying the slightest sign of annoyance or disfavour.

This I considered a triumph of my own diplomacy. Up to a certain point I, as her best friend in those hard, dark days bygone, possessed a complete influence over her. But beyond that, when it became a question involving her father's honour, I was entirely powerless. She was a girl of strong individuality, and like all such, was quick of penetration, and peculiarly subject to prejudice on account of her high sense of honour.

She flattered me by declaring that she wished that I had been appointed her secretary, whereupon I thanked her for the compliment, but asserted—

"Such a thing could never have been."

"Why?"

"Because you have told me that this fellow Dawson is coming here as a matter of right. Your father wrote that unfortunate clause in his will under compulsion—which means, because he stood in fear of him."

"Yes," she sighed in a low voice. "You are right, Mr. Greenwood. Quite right. He held my father's life in his hands."

This latter remark struck me as very strange. Could Burton Blair have been guilty of some nameless crime that he should fear this mysterious one-eyed Englishman? Perhaps so. Perhaps the man Dick

Dawson, who had for years been passing as an Italian in rural Italy, was the only living witness of an incident which Blair, in his prosperous days, would have gladly given a million to efface. Such, indeed, was one of the many theories which arose within me. Yet when I recollected the bluff, good-natured honesty of Burton Blair, his sterling sincerity, his high-mindedness, and his anonymous charitable works for charity's sake, I crushed down all such suspicions, and determined only to respect the dead man's memory.

The next night, just before nine o'clock, as Reggie and I were chatting over our coffee in our cosy little dining-room in Great Russell Street, Glave, our man, tapped, entered, and handed me a card.

I sprang from my chair, as though I had received an electric shock.

"Well! This is funny, old chap," I cried turning to my friend. "Here's actually the man Dawson himself."

"Dawson!" gasped the man against whom the monk had warned me. "Let's have him in. But, by Gad! we must be careful of what we say, for, if all is true of him, he has the cuteness of Old Nick himself."

"Leave him to me," I said. Then turning to Glave, said, "Show the gentleman in."

And we both waited in breathless expectancy for the appearance of the man who knew the truth concerning the carefully-guarded past of Burton Blair, and who, for some mysterious reason, had concealed himself so long in the guise of an Italian.

A moment later he was ushered in, and bowing to us exclaimed with a smile—

"I suppose, gentlemen, I have to introduce myself. My name is Dawson—Richard Dawson."

"And mine is Gilbert Greenwood," I said rather distantly. "While my friend here is Reginald Seton."

"I have heard of you both from our mutual friend, now unfortunately deceased, Burton Blair," he exclaimed; and sank slowly into the grandfather armchair which I indicated, while I myself stood upon the hearthrug with my back to the fire in order to take a good look at him.

He was in well-made evening clothes, over which he wore a black overcoat, yet there was nothing about him suggestive of the man of strong character. He was of middle height, and his age I judged to be nearly fifty. He wore gold-framed round eye-glasses with thick pebbles, through which he seemed to blink at us like a German professor, and his general aspect was that of a sedate and studious man.

Beneath a patchy mass of grey-brown hair his forehead fell in wrinkled notches over a pair of sunken blue eyes, one of which looked upon the world in speculative wonder, while the other was grey, cloudy, and sightless. Straggling eyebrows wandered in a curiously uncertain manner to their meeting-place above a somewhat fleshy nose. Below the cheeks and beard and moustache blended in a colour-scheme of grey. From the sleeves of his overcoat, as he sat there before us, his lithe, brown fingers shot in and out, twisting and tapping the padded arms of the chair with nervous persistence, and in a manner which indicated the high tension of the man.

"My reason for intruding upon you at this hour," he said half apologetically, yet with a mysterious smile upon his thick lips, "is because I only arrived back in London this evening and discovered that my friend Blair has, by his will, left in my hands the control of his daughter's affairs."

"Oh!" I exclaimed in pretended surprise as though it were news to me. "And who has said this?"

"I have received information privately," was his evasive answer. "But before proceeding further, I thought it best to call upon you, in order that we might from the outset thoroughly understand each other. I know that both of you have been Blair's most intimate and kindest friends, while owing to certain somewhat curious circumstances I have been compelled, until to-day, to remain entirely in the background, his friend in secret as it were. I am also well aware of the circumstances in which you met, of your charity to my dead friend and to his daughter— in fact, he told me everything, for he had no secrets from me. Yet you on your part," he continued, glancing at us from one to the other with that single blue eye, "you must have regarded his sudden wealth as a complete mystery."

"We certainly have done," I remarked.

"Ah!" he exclaimed quickly in a tone of ill-concealed satisfaction. "Then he has revealed to you nothing!"

And in an instant I saw that I had inadvertently told the fellow exactly what he most desired to know.

XIII

Burton Blair's Secret is Revealed

"Whatever Burton Blair told me was in strictest confidence," I exclaimed, resenting the fellow's intrusion, yet secretly glad to have that opportunity of meeting him and of endeavouring to ascertain his intentions.

"Of course," answered Dawson with a smile, his one shining eye blinking at me from behind his gold-rimmed glasses. "But his friendliness and gratitude never led him sufficiently far to reveal to you his secret. No. I think if you will pardon me, Mr. Greenwood, it is useless for us to fence in this manner, having regard to the fact that I know rather more of Burton Blair and his past life than you ever have done."

"Admitted," I said. "Blair was always very reticent. He set himself to solve some mystery and achieved his object."

"And by doing so gained over two millions sterling which people still regard as a mystery. There is, however, no mystery about those heaps of securities lying at his banks, nor about the cash with which he purchased them," he laughed. "It was good Bank of England notes and solid gold coin of the realm. But now he's dead, poor fellow; it has all come to an end," he added with a slightly reflective air.

"But his secret still exists," Reggie remarked. "He has bequeathed it to my friend here."

"What!" snapped the man with one eye, turning to me in sheer amazement. "He has left his secret with you?"

He seemed utterly staggered by Reggie's words, and I noted the evil glitter in his glance.

"He has. The secret is now mine," I answered; although I did not tell him that the mysterious little wash leather bag was missing.

"But don't you know what that involves, man?" he cried, and having risen from his chair he now stood before me, his thin fingers twitching with excitement.

"No, I don't," I said, laughing in an endeavour to treat his words lightly. "He has left me as a legacy the little bag he always carried, together with certain instructions which I shall endeavour to act upon."

"Very well," he snarled. "Do just as you think fit, only I would rather you were left possessor of that secret than me—that's all."

His dismay and annoyance apparently knew no bounds. He strove hard to conceal it, but without avail. It was therefore at once plain that there was some very strong motive why the secret should not be allowed to fall into my possession. Yet his belief that the little sachet had already passed into my hands negatived my theory that this mysterious person was in any way connected with Burton Blair's death.

"Believe me, Mr. Dawson," I said quite calmly, "I entertain no fear of the result of my friend's kind generosity. Indeed, I can see no ground for any apprehension. Blair discovered a mystery which, by dint of long patience and almost superhuman effort, he succeeded in solving, and I presume that, possibly from a feeling of some little gratitude for the small help my friend and myself were able to render him, he has left his secret in my keeping."

The man was silent for several moments with that single irritating eye fixed upon me immovably.

"Ah!" he exclaimed at last with impatience. "I see that you are in utter ignorance. Perhaps it is as well that you should remain so." Then he added, "But let us talk of another matter—of the future."

"Well?" I inquired, "and what of the future?"

"I am appointed secretary to Mabel Blair, and the controller of her affairs."

"And I promised Burton Blair upon his deathbed to guard and protect the young lady's interests," I said, in a cold, calm voice.

"Then may I ask, now we are upon the subject, whether you entertain matrimonial intentions towards her?"

"No, you shall not ask me anything of the kind," I blazed forth. "Your question is a piece of outrageous impertinence, sir."

"Come, come, Gilbert," Reggie exclaimed.

"There's surely no need to quarrel."

"None whatever," declared Mr. Richard Dawson, with a supercilious air. "The question is quite simple, and one which I, as the future controller of the young lady's fortune, have a perfect right to ask. I understand," he added, "that she has grown to be very attractive and popular."

"Your question is one which I refuse to answer," I declared with considerable warmth. "I might just as well demand of you the reason why you have been lying low in Italy all these years, or why you received letters addressed to a back street in Florence."

His jaw dropped, his brows slightly contracted, and I saw my remark caused him some apprehension.

"Oh! and how are you aware that I have lived in Italy?"

But in order to mislead him I smiled mysteriously and replied—

"The man who holds Burton Blair's secret also holds certain secrets concerning his friends." Then I added meaningly, "The Ceco is well known in Florence and in Lucca."

His face blanched, his thin, sinewy fingers moved again, and the twitching at the corners of his mouth showed how intensely excited he had become at that mention of his nickname.

"Ah!" he exclaimed. "He has played me false, then, after all—he has told you that—eh? Very well!" And he laughed the strange hollow laugh of a man who contemplates revenge. "Very well, gentlemen. I see my position in this affair is that of an intruder."

"To tell you the truth, sir, it is," exclaimed Reggie. "You were unknown until the dead man's will was read, and I do not anticipate that the young lady will care to be compelled to employ a stranger."

"A stranger!" he laughed, with a haughty touch of sarcasm. "Dick Dawson a stranger! No, sir, you will find that to her I am no stranger. On the other hand you will, I think, discover that instead of resenting my interference, the young lady will rather welcome it. Wait and see," he added, with a strangely confident air. "To-morrow I intend to call upon Mr. Leighton, and to take up my duties as secretary to the daughter of the late Burton Blair, millionaire," and laying stress on the final word, he laughed again defiantly in our faces.

He was not a gentleman. I decided that on the instant he had entered the room. Outwardly his bearing was that of one who had mixed with respectable people, but it was only a veneer of polish, for when he grew excited he was just as uncouth as the bluff seafarer who had so suddenly expired. His twang was pronouncedly Cockney, even though it was said he had lived in Italy so many years that he had almost become an Italian. A man who is a real born Londoner can never disguise his nasal "n's," even though he live his life at the uttermost ends of the earth. We had both quickly detected that the stranger, though of rather slim built, was unusually muscular. And this was the man who had had those frequent secret interviews with the grave-eyed Capuchin, Fra Antonio.

That he stood in no fear of us had been shown by the bold and open manner in which he had called, and the frankness with which he had spoken. He was entirely confident in his own position, and was inwardly chuckling at our own ignorance.

"You speak of me as a stranger, gentlemen," he said, buttoning his overcoat after a short pause and taking up his stick. "I suppose I am to-night—but I shall not be so to-morrow. Very soon, I hope, we shall learn to know one another better, then perhaps you will trust me a little further than you do this evening. Recollect that I have for many years been the dead man's most intimate friend."

It was on the point of my tongue to remark that the reason of the strange clause in the will was because of poor Burton's fear of him, and that it had been inserted under compulsion, but I fortunately managed to restrain myself and to wish the fellow "Good-evening" with some show of politeness.

"Well, I'm hanged, Gilbert," cried Reggie, when the one-eyed man had gone. "The situation grows more interesting and complicated every moment. Leighton has a tough customer to deal with, that's very evident."

"Yes," I sighed. "He has the best of us all round, because Blair evidently took him completely into his confidence."

"Burton treated us shabbily, that's my opinion, Greenwood!" blurted forth my friend, selecting a fresh cigar, and biting off the end viciously.

"He left his secret to me remember."

"He may have destroyed it after making the will," my friend suggested.

"No, it is either hidden or has been stolen—which is not at all plain. For my own part, I consider that the theory of murder is gradually becoming dispelled. If he had any suspicion that he had been the victim of foul play, he surely would have made some remark to us before he died. Of that I feel absolutely convinced."

"Very probably," he remarked, rather dubiously, however. "But what we have now to discover is whether that little bag he wore is still in existence."

"The man Dawson was evidently in England before poor Blair's death. It may have passed into his possession," I suggested.

"He would, in all probability, endeavour to get hold of it," Reggie agreed. "We must establish where he was and what he was doing on that day when Blair was so mysteriously seized in the train. I don't like the fellow, apart from his alias and the secrecy of friendship with Blair. He means mischief, old chap—distinct mischief. I saw it in that one eye of his. Remember what he said about Blair giving him away. It struck me that he contemplates revenge upon poor Mabel."

"He'd better not try to injure her," I exclaimed fiercely. "I've my promise to keep to poor Burton, and I'll keep it—by Heaven, I will!—to the very letter. She sha'n't fall into the hands of that adventurer, I'll take good care."

"She's in fear of him already. I wonder why?"

"Unfortunately she won't tell me. He probably holds some guilty secret of the dead man's, the truth of which, if exposed, might, for all we know, have the effect of placing Mabel herself outside the pale of good society."

Seton grunted, lolled back in his chair, and gazed thoughtfully into the fire.

"By Jove!" he exclaimed, after a brief silence. "I wonder whether that is so?"

On the following morning, as we were seated at breakfast, a note from Mabel was brought by a boy-messenger, asking me to come round to Grosvenor Square at once. Therefore without delay I swallowed my coffee, struggled into my overcoat, and a quarter of an hour later entered the bright morning-room where the dead man's daughter, her face rather flushed by excitement, stood awaiting me.

"What's the matter?" I inquired quickly as I took her hand, fearing that the man she loathed had already called upon her.

"Nothing serious," she laughed. "I have only a piece of very good news for you."

"For me—what?"

Without answering, she placed on the table a small plain silver cigarette-box, upon one corner of the lid of which was engraved the cipher double B, that monogram that was upon all Blair's plate, carriages, harness and other possessions.

"See what is inside that," she exclaimed, pointing to the box before her, and smiling sweetly with profound satisfaction.

I eagerly took it in my hands and raising the lid, peered within.

"What!" I cried aloud, almost beside myself with joy. "It can't really be?"

"Yes," she laughed. "It is."

And then, with trembling fingers, I drew forth from the box the actual object that had been bequeathed to me, the little well-worn bag of chamois leather, the small sachet about the size of a man's palm, attached to which was a thin but very strong golden chain for suspending it around the neck.

"I found it this morning quite accidentally, just as it is, in a secret drawer in the old bureau in my father's dressing-room," she explained. "He must have placed it there for security before leaving for Scotland."

I held it in my hand utterly stupefied, yet with the most profound gratification. Did not the very fact that Blair had taken it off and placed it in that box rather than risk wearing it during that journey to the North prove that he had gone in fear of an attempt being made to obtain its possession? Nevertheless, the curious little object bequeathed to me under such strange conditions was now actually in my hand, a flat, neatly-sewn bag of wash-leather that was black with age and wear, about half-an-inch thick, and containing something flat and hard.

Within was concealed the great secret, the knowledge of which had raised Burton Blair from a homeless seafarer into affluence. What it could be, neither Mabel nor I could for a moment imagine.

Both of us were breathless, equally eager to ascertain the truth. Surely never in the life of any man was there presented a more interesting or a more tantalising problem.

In silence she took up a pair of small buttonhole scissors from the little writing-table in the window and handed them to me.

Then, my hand trembling with excitement, I inserted the point into the end of the leather packet and made a long sharp cut the whole of its length, but what fell out upon the carpet next instant caused us both to utter loud exclamations of surprise.

Burton Blair's most treasured possession, the Great Secret which he had carried on his person all those years and through all those wanderings, now at last revealed, proved utterly astounding.

XIV

Gives an Expert Opinion

Upon the carpet at our feet lay scattered a pack of very small, rather dirty cards which had fallen from the little sachet, and which both of us stood regarding with surprise and disappointment.

For my own part I expected to find within that treasured bag of wash-leather something of more value than those thumbed and half worn-out pieces of pasteboard, but our curiosity was instantly aroused when, on stooping, I picked up one of them and discovered certain letters written in brown faded ink upon it, similar to those upon the card already in my possession.

It chanced to be the ten of diamonds, and in order that you may be able to the more clearly understand the arrangement of the letters upon them, I reproduce it here:—

"How strange!" cried Mabel, taking the card and examining it closely. "It surely must be some cipher, the same as the other card which I found sealed up in the safe."

"No doubt," I exclaimed, as, stooping and gathering up the remainder of the pack, I noticed that upon each of them, either upon the front or upon the back, were scrawled either fourteen or fifteen letters in a treble column, all, of course, utterly unintelligible.

I counted them. It was a piquet pack of thirty-one, the missing card being the ace of hearts which we had already discovered. By the friction of having been carried on the person for so long the corners and edges were worn, while the gloss of the surface had long ago disappeared.

Aided by Mabel I spread them all upon the table, utterly bewildered by the columns of letters which showed that some deep secret was written upon them, yet what it was we were utterly unable to decipher.

Upon the front of the ace of clubs was scrawled in three parallel columns of five letters each, thus:—

```
E   H   N
W   E   D
T   O   L
```

```
I   E   H
W   H   R
```

Again, I turned up the king of spades and found on the reverse only fourteen letters:—

```
Q   W   F
T   S   W
T   H   U
O   F   E
Y   E
```

"I wonder what it all means?" I exclaimed, carefully examining the written characters in the light. The letters were in capitals just as rudely and unevenly drawn as those upon the ace of hearts, evidently by an uneducated hand. Indeed the A's betrayed a foreign form rather than English, and the fact that some of the cards were inscribed on the obverse and others on the reverse seemed to convey some hidden meaning. What it was, however, was both tantalising and puzzling.

"It certainly is very curious," Mabel remarked after she had vainly striven to construct intelligible words from the columns of letters by the easy methods of calculation. "I had no idea that my father carried his secret concealed in this manner."

"Yes," I said, "it really is amazing. No doubt his secret is really written here, if we only knew the key. But in all probability his enemies are aware of its existence, or he would not have left it secreted here when he set forth on his journey to Manchester. That man Dawson may know it."

"Most probably," was her reply. "He was my father's intimate acquaintance."

"His friend—he says he was."

"Friend!" she cried resentfully. "No, his enemy."

"And therefore your father held him in fear? It was that reason which induced him to insert that very injudicious clause in his will."

And then I described to her the visit of the man Dawson on the previous night, telling her what he had said, and his impudent, defiant attitude towards us.

She sighed, but uttered no reply. I noticed that as I spoke her countenance went a trifle paler, but she remained silent, as though she feared to speak lest she should inadvertently expose what she intended should remain a secret.

My chief thought at that moment, however, was the elucidation of the problem presented by those thirty-two well-thumbed cards. The secret of Burton Blair, the knowledge of which had brought him his millions, was hidden there, and as it had been bequeathed to me it was surely to my interest to exert every effort to gain exact knowledge of it. I recollected how very careful he had been over that little bag which now lay empty upon the table, and with what careless confidence he had shown it to me on that night when he was but a homeless wanderer tramping the muddy turnpike roads.

As he had held it in his hand, his eyes had brightened with keen anticipation. He would be a rich man some day, he had prophesied, and I, in my ignorance, had then believed him to be romancing. But when I looked around that room in which I now stood and saw that Murillo and that Tintoretto, each of them worth a small fortune in themselves, I was bound to confess that I had wrongly mistrusted him.

And the secret written upon that insignificant-looking little pack of cards was mine—if only I could decipher it!

Surely no situation could be more tantalising to a poor man like myself. The man whom I had been able to befriend had left me, in gracious recognition, the secret of the source of his enormous income, yet so well concealed was it that neither Mabel nor myself could decipher it.

"What shall you do?" she inquired presently, after poring over the cards in silence for quite ten minutes. "Is there no expert in London who might find out the key? Surely those people who do cryptograms and things could help us?"

"Certainly," was my answer, "but in that case, if they were successful they would discover the secret for themselves."

"Ah, I never thought of that!"

"Your father's directions in his will as to secrecy are very explicit."

"But possession of these cards without the key is surely not of much benefit," she argued. "Could you not consult somebody, and ascertain by what means such records are deciphered?"

"I might make inquiries in a general way," I answered, "but to place the pack of cards blindly in the hands of an expert would, I fear, simply be giving away your father's most confidential possession. There may be written here some fact which it is not desirable that the world shall know."

"Ah!" she said, glancing quickly up at me. "Some facts regarding his past, you mean. Yes. You are quite right, Mr. Greenwood. We must be very careful to guard the secret of these cards well, especially if, as you suggest, the man Dawson really knows the means by which the record may be rendered intelligible."

"The secret has been bequeathed to me, therefore I will take possession of them," I said. "I will also make inquiries, and ascertain by what means such ciphers are rendered into plain English."

I had at that moment thought of a man named Boyle, a professor at a training-college in Leicester who was an expert at anagrams, ciphers, and such things, and I intended to lose no time in running up there to see him and ascertain his opinion.

Therefore at noon I took train at St. Pancras, and about half-past two was sitting with him in his private room at the college. He was a middle-aged, clean-shaven man of quick intelligence, who had frequently won prizes in various competitions offered by different journals; a man who seemed to have committed Bartlett's *Dictionary of Familiar Quotations* to memory, and whose ingenuity in deciphering puzzles was unequalled.

While smoking a cigarette with him, I explained the point upon which I desired his opinion.

"May I see the cards?" he inquired, removing his briar from his mouth and looking at me with some surprise, I thought.

My first impulse was to refuse him sight of them, but on second thoughts I recollected that of all men he was one of the greatest experts in such matters, therefore I drew the little pack from the envelope in which I had placed them.

"Ah!" he exclaimed the moment he took them in his hand and ran quickly through them. "This, Mr. Greenwood, is the most complicated and most difficult of all ciphers. It was in vogue in Italy and Spain in the seventeenth century, and afterwards in England, but seems to have dropped into disuse during the past hundred years or so, probably on account of its great difficulty."

Carefully he spread the cards out in suits upon the table, and seemed to make long and elaborate calculations between the heavy puffs at his pipe.

"No!" he exclaimed. "It isn't what I expected. Guess-work will never help you in this solution. You might try for a hundred years to decipher it, but will fail, if you do not discover the key. Indeed, so much ingenuity is shown in it that a writer in the last century estimated that in such a pack of cards as this, with such a cipher upon them, there are at least fully fifty-two millions of possible arrangements."

"But how is the cipher written?" I inquired much interested, yet with heart-sinking at his inability to assist me.

"It is done in this way," he said. "The writer of the secret settles what he wishes to record and he then arranges the thirty-two cards in what order he wishes. He then writes the first thirty-two letters of his message record, or whatever it may be, on the face or on the back of the thirty-two cards, one letter upon each card consecutively, commencing with the first column, and going on with columns two and three, working down each column, until he has written the last letter of the cipher. In the writing, however, certain prearranged letters are used in place of spaces, and sometimes the cipher is made still more difficult for a chance finder of the cards to decipher by the introduction of a specially arranged shuffle of the cards half way through the writing of the record."

"Very ingenious!" I remarked, utterly bewildered by the extraordinary complication of Burton Blair's secret. "And yet the letters are so plainly written!"

"That's just it," he laughed. "To the eye it is the plainest of all ciphers, and yet one that is utterly unintelligible unless the exact formula in its writing be known. When that is ascertained the solution becomes easy. The cards are rearranged in the order in which they were written upon, and the record or message spelt off, one letter on each card in succession, reading down one column after another and omitting the letter arranged as spaces."

"Ah!" I exclaimed fervently. "How I wish I knew the key."

"Is this a very important secret, then?" asked Boyle.

"Very," I replied. "A confidential matter which has been placed in my hands, and one which I am bound to solve."

"I fear you will never do so unless the key is in existence," was his answer. "It is far too difficult for me to attempt. The complications which are so simply effected in the writing, shield it effectually from any chance solution. Therefore, all endeavours to decipher it without knowledge of the pre-arrangement of the pack must necessarily prove futile."

He replaced the cards in the envelope and handed them back to me, regretting that he could not render me assistance.

"You might try every day for years and years," he declared, "and you would be no nearer the truth. It is too well protected for chance discovery, and is, indeed, the safest and most ingenious cipher ever devised by man's ingenuity."

I remained and took a cup of tea with him, then at half-past four entered the express and returned to London, disappointed at my utterly fruitless errand. What he had explained to me rendered the secret more impenetrable and inscrutable than ever.

XV

Certain Things We Found at Mayvill

M iss Blair, sir," announced Glave next day just before noon, while I was sitting alone in my room in Great Russell Street, smoking vigorously, and utterly bewildered over the problem of the dead man's pack of cards.

I sprang to my feet to welcome Mabel, who in her rich warm furs was looking very dainty and charming.

"I suppose if Mrs. Percival knew I had come here alone, she'd give me a sound lecture against visiting a man's rooms," she said, laughing after I had greeted her and closed the door.

"Well," I said, "it's scarcely the first time you've honoured me with a visit, is it? And surely you need not trouble very much about Mrs. Percival."

"Oh, she really grows more straight-backed every day," Mabel pouted. "I mustn't go here, and I mustn't go there, and she's afraid of me speaking with this man, and the other man is not to be known, and so on. I'm really growing rather sick of it, I can tell you," she declared, seating herself in the chair I had just vacated, unloosing her heavy sable cape, and stretching a neat ankle to the fire.

"But she's been an awfully good friend to you," I argued. "As far as I can see, she's been the most easy-going of chaperons."

"The perfect chaperon is the one who can utterly and effectually efface herself five minutes after entering the room," Mabel declared. "And I will give Mrs. Percival her due, she's never clung on to me at dances, and if she's found me sitting out in a dim corner she has always made it a point to have an urgent call in an opposite direction. Yes," she sighed, "I suppose I oughtn't to grumble when I recollect the snappy old tabbies in whose hands some girls are. There's Lady Anetta Gordon, for instance, and Vi Drummond, both pretty girls out last season, but whose lives are rendered perfect tortures by those two ugly old hags who cart them about. Why, they've both told me they dare not raise their eyes to a man without a snappy lecture next day on polite manners and maiden modesty."

"Well," I said frankly, standing on the hearthrug, and looking down at her handsome figure: "I really don't think you have had much to complain about up to the present. Your poor father was most indulgent, and I'm sure Mrs. Percival, although she may seem rather harsh at times, is only speaking for your own benefit."

"Oh, I know I'm a very wilful girl in your eyes," she exclaimed, with a smile. "You always used to say so when I was at school."

"Well, to tell the truth, you were," I answered quite openly.

"Of course. You men never make allowance for a girl. You assume your freedom with your first long trousers, while we unfortunate girls are not allowed a single moment alone, either inside the house or out of it. No matter whether we be as ugly as Mother Shipton or as beautiful as Venus, we must all of us be tied up to some elder woman, who very often is just as fond of a mild flirtation as the simpering young miss in her charge. Forgive me for speaking so candidly, won't you, Mr. Greenwood, but my opinion is that the modern methods of society are all sham and humbug."

"You're not in a very polite mood to-day, it seems," I remarked, being unable to restrain a smile.

"No, I'm not," she admitted. "Mrs. Percival is so very aggravating. I want to go down to Mayvill this afternoon, and she won't let me go alone."

"Why do you so particularly wish to go there alone?"

She flushed slightly, and appeared for a moment to be confused.

"Oh, well, I don't want to go alone very particularly, you know," she tried to assure me. "It is the foolishness of not allowing me to travel down there like any other girl that I object to. If a maid can take a railway journey alone, why can't I?"

"Because you have the *convenances* of society to respect—the domestic servant need not."

"Then I prefer the lot of the domestic," she declared in a manner which told me that something had annoyed her. For my own part I should have regretted very much if Mrs. Percival had consented to her going down to Herefordshire alone, while it also seemed apparent that she had some secret reason of her own for not taking her elder companion with her.

What, I wondered, could it be?

I inquired the reason why she wished to go to Mayvill without even a maid, but she made an excuse that she wanted to see the other four hunters were being properly treated by the studs-man, and also to make a search through her father's study to ascertain whether any important or confidential papers remained there. She had the keys, and intended to do this before that odious person, Dawson, assumed his office.

This suggestion, evidently made as an excuse, struck me as one that really should be acted upon without delay, yet it was so very plain that she desired to go alone that at first I hesitated to offer to accompany her. Our friendship was of such a close and intimate character that I could of course offer to do so without overstepping the bounds of propriety, nevertheless I resolved to first endeavour to learn the reason of her strong desire to travel alone.

She was a clever woman, however, and had no intention of telling me. She had a strong and secret desire to go down alone to that fine old country house that was now her own, and did not desire that Mrs. Percival should accompany her.

"If you are really going to search the library, Mabel, had I not better accompany and help you?" I suggested presently. "That is, of course, if you will permit me," I added apologetically.

For a moment she was silent, as though devising some means out of a dilemma, then she answered—

"If you'll come, I'll of course be only too delighted. Indeed, you really ought to assist me, for we might discover some key to the cipher on the cards. My father was down there for three days about a fortnight before his death."

"When shall we start?"

"At three-thirty from Paddington. Will that suit you? You shall come and be my guest." And she laughed mischievously at such utter break-up of the *convenances* and the probable chagrin of the long-suffering Mrs. Percival.

"Very well," I agreed; and ten minutes later I went down with her and put her, smiling sweetly, into her smart victoria, the servants of which were now in mourning.

You perceive that I was playing a very dangerous game? And so I was; as you will afterwards see.

At the hour appointed I met her at Paddington, and putting aside her sad thoughtfulness at her bereavement we travelled together down to Dunmore Station, beyond Hereford. Here we entered the brougham awaiting us, and after a drive of nearly three miles, descended before the splendid old mansion which Burton Blair had bought two years before for the sake of the shooting and fishing surrounding it.

Standing in its fine park half-way between King's Pyon and Dilwyn, Mayvill Court was, and is still, one of the show places of the county. It was an ideal ancestral hall. The grand old gabled house with its lofty square

WILLIAM LE QUEUX

towers, its Jacobean entrance, gateway and dovecote, and the fantastically clipped box-trees and sun-dial of its quaint old-fashioned garden, possessed a delightful charm which few other ancient mansions could boast, and a still further interesting feature lay in its perfectly unaltered state throughout, even to the minutest detail. For close on three hundred years it had been held by its original owners, the Baddesleys, until Blair had purchased it—furniture, pictures, armour, everything just as it stood.

It was nearly nine o'clock when Mrs. Gibbons, the elderly housekeeper, welcomed us, in tears at the death of her master, and we passed into the great oak-panelled hall in which hung the sword and portrait of the gallant cavalier. Captain Harry Baddesley, of whom there still was told a romantic story. Narrowly escaping from the battle-field, the captain spurred homewards, with some of Cromwell's soldiers close at his heels; and his wife, a lady of great courage, had scarcely concealed him in the secret chamber when the enemy arrived to search the house. Little daunted, the lady assisted them and personally conducted them over the mansion. As in so many instances, the secret room was entered from the principal bedroom, and in inspecting the latter the Roundheads had their suspicions aroused. So they decided to stay the night.

The hunted man's wife sent them an ample supper and some wine which had been carefully drugged, with the result that the unwelcome visitors were very soon soundly asleep, and the gallant captain, before the effects of the wine had worn off, were far beyond their reach.

Since that day the old place had remained absolutely unchanged, with its rows of dark, time-mellowed family portraits in the big hall, its Jacobean furniture and its old helmets and pikes that had borne the brunt of Naseby. The night was bitterly cold. In the great open hearth huge logs were blazing, and as we stood there to warm ourselves after our journey, Mrs. Gibbons, who had been apprised of our advent by telegraph, announced that she had prepared supper for us as she knew we could not arrive in time for dinner.

Both she and her husband expressed the deepest sympathy with Mabel in her bereavement, and then having removed our coats we went on into the small dining-room, where supper was served by Gibbons and the footman with that old-fashioned stateliness characteristic of all in that fine old-world mansion.

Gibbons and his wife, old retainers of the former owners, were, I think, somewhat surprised that I had accompanied their young mistress alone, nevertheless Mabel had explained to them how she wished to make a search of her father's effects in the library, and that for that reason she had invited me to accompany her. Yet I must confess that I, on my part, had not yet formed any conclusion as to the real reason of her visit. That there was some ulterior motive in it I felt certain, but what it was I could not even guess.

After supper Mrs. Gibbons took my pretty companion to her room, while Gibbons showed me the one prepared for me, a long big chamber on the first floor, from the windows of which I had a wide view over the undulating lawns to Wormsley Hill and Sarnesfield. I had occupied the room on several occasions, and knew it well, with its great old carved four-poster bed, antique hangings, Jacobean chests and polished oaken ceiling.

After a wash I rejoined my dainty little hostess in the library—a big, long, old room, where a fire burned brightly and the lamps were softly shaded with yellow silk. Over the fireplace were carved in stone the three water-bougets of the Baddesleys, with the date 1601, while the whole room from end to end was lined with brown-backed books that had probably not been disturbed for half-a-century.

After Mabel had allowed me a cigarette and told Gibbons that she did not wish to be disturbed for an hour or so, she rose and turned the key behind the servants, so that we might carry out the work of investigation without interruption.

"Now," she said, turning her fine eyes upon me with an excitement she could not suppress as she walked to the big writing-table and took her father's keys from her pocket, "I wonder whether we shall discover anything of interest. I suppose," she added, "it is really Mr. Leighton's duty to do this. But I prefer that you and I should look into my father's affairs prior to the inquisitive lawyer's arrival."

It almost seemed as if she half-expected to discover something which she desired to conceal from the solicitor.

The dead man's writing-table was a ponderous old-fashioned one of carved oak, and as she unlocked the first drawer and turned out its contents, I drew up chairs and settled with her in order to make a methodical and thorough examination. The papers, we found, were mostly letters from friends, and correspondence from solicitors and brokers regarding his investments in various quarters. From some which I read I gathered what enormous profits he had made over certain deals in Kaffirs, while in certain other correspondence were allusions to matters which, to me, were very puzzling.

Mabel's eager attitude was that of one in search of some document or other which she believed to be there. She scarcely troubled to read any of the letters, merely scanning them swiftly and casting them aside. Thus we examined the contents of one drawer after another until I saw beneath her hand a blue foolscap envelope sealed with black wax, and bearing the superscription in her father's handwriting:—

"To be opened by Mabel after my death.

Burton Blair

"Ah!" she gasped in breathless haste. "I wonder what this contains?" And she eagerly broke the seals, and drew forth a sheet of foolscap closely written, to which some other papers were attached by means of a brass fastener.

From the envelope, too, something fell, and I picked it up, finding to my surprise that it was a snap-shot photograph much worn and tattered, but preserved by being mounted upon a piece of linen. It was a half-faded view of a country crossroads in a flat and rather dismal country, with a small lonely house, probably once an old toll-house, with high chimneys standing on the edge of the highway, a small strip of flower-garden railed off at the side. Before the door was a rustic porch covered by climbing roses, and out on the roadside an old Windsor armchair that had apparently just been vacated.

While I was examining the view beneath the lamp-light, the dead man's daughter was reading swiftly through those close lines her father had penned.

Suddenly she uttered a loud cry as though horrified by some discovery, and, startled, I turned to glance at her. Her countenance had changed; she was blanched to the lips.

"No!" she gasped hoarsely. "I—I can't believe it—I won't!"

Again she glanced at the paper to re-read those fateful lines.

"What is it?" I inquired anxiously. "May I not know?" And I crossed to where she stood.

"No," she answered firmly, placing the paper behind her. "No! Not even you may know this!" And with a sudden movement she tore the paper to pieces in her hands, and ere I could rescue it, she had cast the fragments into the fire.

The flames leapt up, and next instant the dead man's confession—if such it were—was consumed and lost for ever, while his daughter stood, haggard, rigid and white as death.

XVI

In which Two Curious Facts are Established

Mabel's sudden action both annoyed and surprised me, for I had believed that our friendship was of such a close and intimate character that she would at least have allowed me sight of what her father had written.

Yet when, next second, I reflected that the envelope had been specially addressed to her, I saw that whatever was contained therein had been intended for her eye alone.

"You have discovered something which has upset you?" I said, looking straight into her white, hard-drawn face. "I hope it is really nothing very disconcerting?"

She held her breath for a moment, her hand instinctively upon her breast as though to still the wild beating of her heart.

"Ah! unfortunately it is," was her answer. "I know the truth now—the awful, terrible truth." And without a word of warning she covered her face with her hands and burst into a torrent of tears.

At her side in an instant I was striving to console her, but I quickly realised what a deep impression of dismay and horror those written words of her dead father had produced upon her. She was filled with grief, and utterly inconsolable.

The quiet of that long, old-fashioned room was unbroken save for her bitter sobs and the solemn tick-tock of the antique grandfather clock at the further end of the apartment. My hand was placed tenderly upon the poor girl's shoulder, but it was a long time ere I could induce her to dry her tears.

When she did so, I saw by her face that she had become a changed woman.

Walking back to the writing-table she took up the envelope and re-read the superscription which Blair had written upon it, and then for the first time her eyes fell upon the photograph of that lonely house by the crossways.

"Why!" she cried, startled, "where did you find this?"

I explained that it had dropped from the envelope, whereupon she took it up and gazed, for a long time upon it. Then, turning it over, she discovered what I had not noticed, namely, written faintly in pencil and half effaced were the words, "Owston crossroads, 9 miles beyond Doncaster on the Selby Road.—B. B."

"Do you know what this is?"

"No, I haven't the least idea," I answered. "It must be something of which your father was very careful. It seems to be well worn, too, as though carried in somebody's pocket."

"Well," she said, "I will tell you. I had no idea that he still preserved it, but I suppose he kept it as a souvenir of those weary journeys of long ago. This photograph," she added, holding it still in her hand, "is the picture of the spot for which he searched every turnpike in England. He had the photograph but nothing else to guide him to the spot, and we were therefore compelled to tramp all the main roads up and down the country in an attempt to identify it. Not until nearly a year after you and Mr. Seton had so kindly placed me at school at Bournemouth did my father, still on his lonely tramp, succeed in discovering it after a search lasting over three years. He identified it one summer evening as the crossways at Owston, and he found living in that house the person of whom he had been all those weary months in search."

"Curious," I said. "Tell me more about it."

"There is nothing else to tell, except that, by identifying the house, he obtained the key to the secret—at least, that is what I always understood from him," she said. "Ah, I recollect all those long wearying walks when I was a girl, how we trudged on over those long, white, endless roads, in sunshine and in rain, envying people in carriages and carts, and men and women on bicycles, and yet my courage always supported by my father's declaration that great fortune must be ours some day. He carried this photograph with him always, and almost at each crossroad he would take it out, examine the landscape and compare it, not knowing, of course, but that the old toll-house might have been pulled down since the taking of the picture."

"Did he never tell you the reason why he wished to visit that house."

"He used to say that the man who lived there—the man who used to sit on summer evenings in that chair outside, was his friend—his good friend; only they had been parted for a long time, and he did not know that my father was still alive. They had been friends abroad, I fancy, in the days when my father was at sea."

"And the identification of this spot was the reason of your father's constant wanderings?" I exclaimed, pleased that I had at last cleared up one point which, for five years or so, had been a mystery.

"Yes. A month after he had made the discovery he came to Bournemouth, and told me in confidence that his dream of great wealth was about to be realised. He had solved the problem, and within a week or two would be in possession of ample funds. He disappeared, you will remember, almost immediately, and was away for a month. Then he returned a rich man—so rich that you and Mr. Seton were utterly dumbfounded. Don't you recollect that night at Helpstone, after I had come from school to spend a week with my father on his return? We were sitting together after dinner and poor father recalled the last occasion when we had all assembled there—the occasion when I was taken ill outside," she added. "And don't you recollect Mr. Seton appearing to doubt my father's statement that he was already worth fifty thousand pounds."

"I remember," I answered, as her clear eyes met mine. "I remember how your father struck us utterly dumb by going upstairs and fetching his banker's pass-book, which showed a balance of fifty-four thousand odd pounds. After that he became more than ever a mystery to us. But tell me," I added in a low, earnest voice, "what have you discovered to-night that has so upset you?"

"I have nearly found proof of a fact that I have dreaded for years—a fact that affects not only my poor father's memory, but also myself. I am in peril—personal danger."

"How?" I asked quickly, failing to understand her meaning. "Recollect that I promised your father to act as your protector."

"I know, I know. It is awfully good of you," she said, looking at me gratefully with those wonderful eyes that had always held me fascinated beneath the spell of her beauty. "But," she added, shaking her head sorrowfully, "I fear that in this you will be powerless. If the blow falls, as it must sooner or later, then I shall be crushed and helpless. No power, not even your devoted friendship, can then save me."

"You certainly speak very strangely, Mabel. I don't follow you at all."

"I expect not," was her mechanical answer. "You do not know all. If you did, you would understand the peril of my position and of the great danger now threatening me."

And she stood motionless as a statue, her hand upon the corner of the writing-table, her eyes fixed straight into the blazing fire.

"If the danger is a real one, I consider I ought to be aware of it. To be forewarned is to be forearmed!" I remarked decisively.

"It is a real one, but as my father has confessed the truth to me alone, I am unable to reveal it to you. His secret is mine."

"Certainly," I answered, accepting her decision, which, of course, was but natural in the circumstances. She could not betray her dead father's confidence.

Yet if she had done, how altered would have been the course of events! Surely the story of Burton Blair was one of the strangest and most romantic ever given to man to relate, and as assuredly the strange circumstances which occurred after his decease were even more remarkable and puzzling. The whole affair from beginning to end was a complete enigma.

Later, when Mabel grew slightly calmer, we concluded our work of investigation, but discovered little else of interest save several letters in Italian, undated and unsigned, but evidently written by Dick Dawson, the millionaire's mysterious friend—or enemy. On reading them they were, I found, evidently the correspondence of an intimate acquaintance who was sharing Blair's fortune and secretly assisting him in the acquisition of his wealth. There was much mention of "the secret," and repeated cautions against revealing anything to Reggie or to myself.

In one letter I found the sentences in Italian: "My girl is growing into quite a fine lady. I expect she will become a Countess, or perhaps a Duchess, one day. I hear from your side that Mabel is becoming a very pretty woman. You ought, with your position and reputation, to make a good match for her. But I know what old-fashioned ideas you hold that a woman must marry only for love."

On reading this, one fact was vividly impressed upon me, namely, that if this man Dawson shared secretly in Blair's wealth he surely had no necessity to obtain his secret by foul means, when he already knew it.

The clock on the stables chimed midnight before Mabel rang for Mrs. Gibbons, and the latter's husband followed, bringing me a night-cap of whisky and some hot water.

My little companion merrily pressed my hand, wishing me good-night, and then retired, accompanied by the housekeeper, while Gibbons himself remained to mix my drink.

"Sad thing, sir, about our poor master," hazarded the well-trained servant, who had been all his life in the service of the previous owners. "I fear the poor young mistress feels it very much."

"Very much indeed, Gibbons," I answered, taking a cigarette and standing with my back to the fire. "She was such a devoted daughter."

"She is now mistress of everything, Mr. Ford told us when he was down three days ago."

"Yes," I said, "everything. And I hope that you and your wife will serve her as well and as faithfully as you have done her father."

"We'll try, sir," was the grave, grey-haired man's response. "Everybody's very fond of the young mistress. She's so very good to all the servants." Then, as I remained silent, he placed my candle in readiness on the table, and, bowing, wished me good-night.

He closed the door, and I was alone in that great silent old room where the darting flames cast weird lights across into the dark recesses, and the long, old Chippendale clock ticked on solemnly as it had done for a century past.

Having swallowed my hot drink, I returned again to my dead friend's writing-table, carefully examining it to see whether it contained any secret drawers. A methodical investigation of every portion failed to reveal any spring or unsuspected cavity, therefore, after glancing at that photograph which had taken Blair those many months of weary tramping to identify, I extinguished the lamps and passing through the great old hall with the stands of armour which conjured up visions of ghostly cavaliers, ascended to my room.

The bright fire gave the antique place with those rather funereal hangings a warm and cosy appearance in contrast to the hard frost outside, and feeling no inclination to sleep just then, I flung myself into an arm-chair and sat with arms folded, pondering deeply.

Again the stable-clock chimed—the half-hour—and then I think I must have dozed, for I was awakened suddenly by a light, stealthy footstep on the polished oaken floor outside my door. I listened, and distinctly heard some one creeping lightly down the big old Jacobean staircase, which creaked slightly somewhere below.

The weird ghostliness of the old place and its many historic traditions caused me, I suppose, some misgivings, for I found myself thinking of burglars and of midnight visitants. Again I strained my ears. Perhaps, after all, it was only a servant! Yet, when I glanced at my watch, and found it to be a quarter to two, the suggestion that the servants had not retired was at once negatived.

Suddenly, in the room below me, I distinctly heard a slow, harsh, grating noise. Then all was still again.

About three minutes later, however, I fancied I heard low whispering, and, having quickly extinguished my light, I drew aside one of my heavy curtains, and peering forth saw, to my surprise, two figures crossing the lawn towards the shrubbery.

The moon was somewhat overcast, yet by the grey, clouded light I distinguished that the pair were a man and a woman. From the man's back I could not recognise him, but his companion's gait was familiar to me as she hurried on towards the dark belt of bare, black trees.

It was Mabel Blair. The secret was out. Her sudden desire to visit Mayvill was in order to keep a midnight tryst.

XVII

Merely Concerns a Stranger

Without a moment's hesitation I struggled into an overcoat, slipped on a golf cap and sped downstairs to the room below my own, where I found one of the long windows open, and through it stepped quickly out upon the gravel.

I intended to discover the motive of this meeting and the identity of her companion—evidently some secret lover whose existence she had concealed from us all. Yet to follow her straight across the lawn in the open light was to at once court detection. Therefore I was compelled to take a circuitous course, hugging the shadows always, until I at length reached the shrubbery, where I halted, listening eagerly.

There was no sound beyond the low creaking of the branches and the dismal sighing of the wind. A distant train was passing through the valley, and somewhere away down in the village a collie was barking. I could not, however, distinguish any human voices. Slowly I made my way through the fallen leaves until I had skirted the whole of the shrubbery, and then I came to the conclusion that they must have passed through it by some bypath and gone out into the park.

My task was rendered more difficult because the moon was not sufficiently overcast to conceal my movements, and I feared that by emerging into the open I might betray my presence.

But Mabel's action in coming there to meet this man, whoever he was, puzzled me greatly. Why had she not met him in London? I wondered. Could he be such an unpresentable lover that a journey to London was impossible? It is not an uncommon thing for a well-born girl to fall in love with a labourer's son any more than it is for a gentleman to love a peasant girl. Many a pretty girl in London to-day has a secret admiration for some young labourer or good-looking groom on her father's estate, the seriousness of the unspoken love lying in the utter impossibility of its realisation.

With ears and eyes open I went on, taking advantage of all the shadow I could, but it seemed as though, having nearly five minutes' start of me, they had taken a different direction to that which I believed.

At last I gained the comparative gloom of the old beech avenue which led straight down to the lodge on the Dilwyn road, and continued along it for nearly half-a-mile, when suddenly my heart leaped for joy, for I distinguished before me the two figures walking together and engaged in earnest conversation.

My jealous anger was in an instant aroused. Fearing that they might hear my footsteps on the hard frozen road I slipped outside the trees upon the grass of the park, and treading noiselessly was soon able to approach almost level with them without attracting attention.

Presently, on the old stone bridge across the river which formed the outlet of the lake, they halted, when, concealing myself behind a tree, I was enabled, by the light of the moon which had fortunately now grown brighter, to clearly see the features of Mabel's mysterious companion. I judged him to be about twenty-eight, an ill-bred, snub-nosed, yellow-haired common-looking fellow, whose hulking form as he leaned against the low parapet was undoubtedly that of an agriculturist. His face was hard-featured and prematurely weather-beaten, while the cut of his clothes was distinctly that of the "ready-made" emporium of the provincial town. His hard felt hat was cocked a little askew, as is usual with the yokel as well as with the costermonger when he takes his Sunday walk.

As far as I could observe he seemed to be treating her with extraordinary disdain and familiarity, addressing her as "Mab" and lighting a cheap cigarette in her presence, while on her part she seemed rather ill at ease, as though she were there under compulsion rather than by choice.

She had dressed herself warmly in a thick frieze driving cape and a close-fitting peaked cap which, drawn over her eyes, half-concealed her features.

"I really can't see your object, Herbert," I heard her distinctly argue. "What could such an action possibly benefit you?"

"A lot," the fellow answered, adding in a rough, uncouth voice which bore the unmistakable brogue of the countryman, "What I say I mean. You know that, don't yer?"

"Of course," she answered. "But why do you treat me in this manner? Think of the risks I run in meeting you here to-night. What would people think if it were known?"

"What do I care what people think!" he exclaimed carelessly. "Of course you've got to keep up appearances—fortunately, I ain't."

"But you surely won't do what you threaten?" she exclaimed in a voice of blank dismay. "Remember that our secrets have been mutual. I have never betrayed you—never in any single thing."

"No, because you knew what would be the result if you did," he laughed with a sneer. "I never trust a woman's word—I don't. You're rich now the old man's dead, and I want money," he said decisively.

"But I haven't any yet," she replied. "When will you have some?"

"I don't know. There are all sorts of law formalities to go through before, so Mr. Greenwood says."

"Oh! a curse on Greenwood!" the fellow burst forth. "He's always with you up in London, they say. Ask him to get you some money from the lawyers. Tell him you're hard up—got to pay bills, or something. Any lie will do for him."

"Impossible, Herbert," she answered, trying to remain calm. "You must really be patient."

"Oh, yes, I know!" he cried. "Call me good dog and all that. But that kind of game don't suit me—you hear? I've got no money, and I must have some at once—tonight."

"I haven't any," she declared.

"But you've got lots of jewellery and plate and stuff. Give me some of that, and I can sell it easily in Hereford to-morrow. Where's that diamond bracelet the old man gave you for a present last birthday—the one you showed me?"

"Here," she replied, and raised her wrist, showing him the beautiful diamond and sapphire ornament her father had given her, the worth of which was two hundred pounds at the very least.

"Give me that," he said. "It'll last me a day or two until you get me some cash."

She hesitated, evidently indisposed to accede to such a request and more especially as the bracelet was the last present her father had made her. Yet, when he repeated his demands in a more threatening tone, it became plain that the fellow's influence was supreme, and that she was as helpless as a child in his unscrupulous hands.

The situation came upon me as an absolute revelation. I could only surmise that a harmless flirtation in the years before her affluence had developed into this common fellow presuming upon her good nature, and, finding her generous and sympathetic, he had now assumed an attitude of mastery over her actions. The working of the rustic mind is most difficult to follow. To-day in rural England there is so very little real gratitude shown by the poor towards the rich that in the country districts, charity is almost entirely unappreciated, while the wealthy are becoming weary of attempting to please or improve the people. Your rustic of to-day, while perfectly honest in his dealings with his own class, cannot resist dishonesty when selling his produce or his labour to the rich man. It seems part of his religion to get, by fair means or by foul, as much as he can out of the gentleman, and then abuse him in the village ale-house and dub him a fool for allowing himself to be thus cheated. Much as I regret to allege it, nevertheless it is a plain and bitter truth that swindling and immorality are the two most notable features of English village life at the present moment.

I stood listening to that strange conversation between the millionaire's daughter and her secret lover, immovable and astounded.

The arrogance of the fellow caused my blood to boil. A dozen times as he sneered at her insultingly, now cajoling, now threatening, and now making a disgusting pretence of affection, I felt impelled to rush out and give him a good sound hiding. It was, indeed, only because I recognised that in this affair, so serious was it, I could only assist Mabel by remaining concealed and using my knowledge of it to her advantage that I held my tongue and stayed my hand.

Without doubt she had, in her girlish inexperience, once believed herself in love with the fellow, but now the hideousness of the present situation was presented to her in all its vivid reality and she saw herself hopelessly involved. Probably it was with a vain hope of extricating herself that she had kept the appointment; but, in any case, the man whom she called Herbert was quick to detect that he held all the honours in the game.

"Now come," he said at last, in his broad brogue, "if you really ain't got no money on you, hand over that bracelet and ha' done with it. We don't want to wait 'ere all night, for I've got to be in Hereford first thing in the morning. So the least said the better."

I saw that, white to the lips, she was trembling in fear of him, for she shrank from his touch, crying—

"Ah, Herbert, it is too cruel of you—too cruel—after all I've done to help you. Have you no pity, no compassion?"

"None," he growled. "I want money and must have it. In a week you must pay me a thousand quid—you hear that, don't you?"

"But how can I? Wait and I'll give it to you later—indeed, I promise."

"I tell you I ain't going to be fooled," he cried angrily. "I mean to have the money, or else I'll blow the whole thing. Then where will you be—eh?" And he laughed a hard triumphant laugh, while she shrank back pale, breathless and dismayed.

I clenched my fists, and to this moment I do not know how I restrained myself from springing from my hiding-place and knocking the fellow down. At that moment I could have killed him where he stood.

"Ah!" she cried, her hands clasped to him in a gesture of supplication, "you surely don't mean what you say, you can't mean that, you really can't! You'll spare me, won't you? Promise me!"

"No, I won't spare you," was his brutal reply, "unless you pay me well."

"I will, I will," she assured him in a low, hoarse voice, which was eminently that of a desperate woman, terrified lest some terrible secret of hers should be exposed.

"Ah!" he sneered with curling lip, "you treated me with contempt once, because you were a fine lady, but I am yet to have my revenge, as you will see. You are now mistress of a great fortune, and I tell you quite plainly that I intend you to share it with me. Act just as you think best, but recollect what refusal will mean to you—exposure!"

"Ah!" she cried desperately, "to-night you have revealed yourself in your true light! You brute, you would, without the slightest compunction, ruin me!"

"Because, my dear girl, you are not playing straight," was his cool, arrogant reply. "You thought that you had most ingeniously got rid of me for ever, until to-night here I am, you see, back again, ready to— well, to be pensioned off, shall we call it? Don't think I intend to allow you to fool me this time, so just give me the bracelet as a first instalment, and say no more." And he snatched at her arm while she, by a quick movement, avoided him.

"I refuse," she cried with a fierce and sudden determination. "I know you now! You are brutal and inhuman, without a speck of either love or esteem—a man who would drive a woman to suicide in order to get money. Now you have been released from prison you intend to live upon me—your letter with that proposal is sufficient proof. But I tell you here to-night that you will obtain not a penny more from me beyond the money that is now paid you every month."

"To keep my mouth closed," he interrupted. And I saw an evil, murderous glitter in his black eyes.

"You need not keep it closed any longer," she said in open defiance. "Indeed, I shall tell the truth myself, and thus put an end to this brilliant blackmailing scheme of yours. So now you understand," she added firmly, with a courage that was admirable.

A silence fell between them for a moment, broken only by the weird cry of an owl.

"Then that is absolutely your decision, eh?" he inquired in a hard voice, while I noticed that his face was white with anger and chagrin as he recognised that, if she told the truth and faced the consequence of her own exposure, whatever it might be, his power over her would be dispelled.

"My mind is made up. I have no fear of any exposure you may make concerning me."

"At any rate give me that bracelet," he demanded savagely, with set teeth, grasping her arm and trying by force to undo the clasp.

"Let me go!" she cried. "You brute! Let me go! Would you rob me, as well as insult me?"

"Rob you!" he muttered, his coarse white face wearing a dangerous expression of unbridled hatred, "rob you!" he hissed with a ford oath, "I'll do more. I'll put you where your cursed tongue won't wag again, and where you won't be able to tell the truth!"

And, unfortunately, before I was aware of his intentions he had seized her by the wrists and, with a quick movement, forced her backwards so violently against the low parapet of the bridge that for a moment they stood locked in a deadly embrace.

Mabel screamed on realising his intentions, but next second with a vile imprecation he had forced her backwards over the low wall, and with a loud splash she fell helplessly into the deep, dark waters.

In an instant, while the fellow took to his heels, I dashed forward to her rescue, but, alas! too late, for, as I peered eagerly down into the darkness, I saw to my dismay that the swirling icy flood had closed over her, that she had disappeared.

XVIII

THE CROSSWAYS AT OWSTON

The sound of the assassin's fast-receding footsteps, as he escaped away down the dark avenue towards the road, awakened me to a keen sense of my responsibility, and in an instant I had divested myself of my overcoat and coat, and stood peering anxiously into the darkness beneath the bridge.

Those seconds seemed hours, until of a sudden I caught sight of a flash of white in mid stream, and without a moment's hesitation I dived in after it.

The shock of the icy water was a severe one but, fortunately, I am a strong swimmer, and neither the intense coldness nor the strength of the current interfered much with my progress as I struck out towards the unconscious girl. Having seized her, however, I had to battle severely to prevent being swept out around the bend where I, knew that the river, joined by another stream, broadened out, and where any chances of effecting a rescue would be very small.

For some minutes I struggled with all my might to hold the unconscious girl's head above the surface, yet so strong was the swirling flood, with its lumps of floating ice, that all resistance seemed impossible, and we were both swept down for some distance until at last, summoning my last effort I managed to strike out with my senseless burden and reach a shallow, where I managed by dint of fierce struggling, to land and to drag the unfortunate girl up the frozen bank.

I had once, long ago, attended an ambulance class, and now, acting upon the instructions I had there received, I set at once to work to produce artificial respiration. It was heavy work alone, with my wet clothes freezing stiff upon me, but still I persevered, determined, if possible, to restore her to consciousness, and this I was fortunately able to do within half an hour.

At first she could utter no word, and I did not question her. Sufficient was it for me to know that she was still alive, for when first I had brought her to land I believed that she was beyond human aid, and that the dastardly attempt of her low-born lover had been successful. She shivered from head to foot, for the night wind cut like a knife, and presently, at my suggestion, she rose and, leaning heavily upon my arm, tried to walk. The attempt was at first only a feeble one, but presently she quickened her pace slightly and, without either of us mentioning what had occurred, I conducted her up the long avenue back to the house. Once within she declared that it was unnecessary to call Mrs. Gibbons. In low whispers she implored me to remain silent upon what had occurred. She took my hand in hers and held it.

"I want you, if you will, to forget all that has transpired," she said, deeply in earnest. "If you followed me and overheard what passed between us, I want you to consider that those words have never been uttered. I—I want you to—" she faltered and then paused without concluding her sentence.

"What do you wish me to do?" I inquired, after a brief and painful silence.

"I want you to still regard me with some esteem, as you always have done," she said, bursting into tears, "I don't like to think that I've fallen in your estimation. Remember, I am a woman—and may be forgiven a woman's impulses and follies."

"You have not fallen in my estimation at all, Mabel," I assured her. "My only regret is that the scoundrel made such an outrageous attempt upon you. But it was fortunate that I followed you, although I suppose I ought to apologise to you for acting the eavesdropper."

"You saved my life," was her whispered answer, as she pressed my hand in thanks. Then she crept swiftly and silently up the big staircase and was lost to view.

Next morning she appeared at the breakfast-table, looking apparently little the worse for her narrow escape, save perhaps that around her eyes were dark rings that told of sleeplessness and terrible anxiety. But she nevertheless chatted merrily, as though no care weighed upon her mind. While Gibbons was in the room serving us she could not speak confidentially, but as she looked across at me, her glance was full of meaning.

At last, when we had finished and had walked together across the great hall back to the library, I said to her—

"Shall you allow the regrettable incident of last night to pass unnoticed? If you do, I fear that man may make another attempt upon you. Therefore it will surely be better if he understands once and for all that I was a witness of his dastardly cowardice."

"No," she replied in a low, pained voice. "Please don't let us discuss it. It must pass."

"Why?"

"Because if I were to seek to punish him he might bring forward something—something that I wish kept secret."

I knew that, I recollected every word of that heated conversation. The blackmailer held some secret of hers which, being detrimental, she dreaded might be revealed.

Surely it was all a strange and most remarkable enigma from beginning to end! From that winter night on the highway near Helpstone, when I had found her fallen at the wayside, until that very moment, mystery had piled upon mystery and secret upon secret until, with Burton Blair's decease and with the pack of tiny cards he had so curiously bequeathed to me, the problem had assumed gigantic proportions.

"That man would have murdered you, Mabel," I said. "You are is fear of him?"

"I am," she answered simply, her gaze fixed across the lawn and park beyond, and she sighed.

"But ought you not to assume the defensive now that the fellow has deliberately endeavoured to take your life?" I argued. "His villainous action last night was purely criminal!"

"It was," she said in a blank, hollow voice, turning her eyes upon me. "I had no idea of his intention. I confess that I came down here because he compelled me to meet him. He has heard of my father's death and now realises that he can obtain money from me; that I shall be forced to yield to his demands."

"You may surely tell me his name," I said.

"Herbert Hales," she replied, not, however, without some hesitation. Then she added, "But I do wish Mr. Greenwood, you would do me a favour and not mention the painful affair again. You do not know how it upsets me, or how much depends upon that man's silence."

I promised, although before doing so I tried my level best to induce her to give me some clue to the nature of the secret held by the uncouth yokel. But she was still obdurate and refused to tell me anything.

That the secret was something which affected herself or her own honour seemed quite plain, for, at every suggestion of mine to bring the fellow face to face with her, she shrank in fear of the startling revelation he could make.

I wondered whether that document, for her eyes only, which had been written by the man now dead, and which she had destroyed on the previous night, had any connexion with the secret known by Herbert Hales. Indeed, whatever the nature of that fellow's knowledge, it was potent enough to compel her to travel down from London in order, if possible, I supposed, to arrange terms with him.

Fortunately, however, the household at Mayvill was unaware of the events of the previous night, and when at midday we left again to return to London, Gibbons and his wife stood at the door and wished us both a pleasant journey.

The house steward and his wife of course believed that the object of our flying visit was to search the dead man's effects, and with the natural curiosity of servants, both were eager to know whether we had discovered anything of interest, although they were unable to question us directly. Inquisitiveness increases with a servant's trustworthiness, until the confidential servant usually knows as much of his master's or mistress' affairs as they do themselves. Burton Blair had been particularly fond of the Gibbonses, and it almost seemed as though the latter considered themselves slighted by not being informed of every disposition made by their dead master in his will.

As it was, we only told them of one, the legacy of two hundred pounds apiece, which Blair had left them, and this had of course caused them the most profound gratification.

Having deposited Mabel at Grosvenor Square, and taken lingering leave of her, I returned at once to Great Russell Street and found that Reggie had just returned from the warehouse in Cannon Street.

Acting upon my sweet little friend's appeal I told him nothing of the exciting incident of the previous night. All I explained was the searching of Blair's writing-table and what we had discovered there.

"Well, we ought I think to go and see that house by the crossways," he said when he had seen the photograph. "Doncaster is a quick run from King's Cross. We could get there and back to-morrow. I'm interested to see the house to discover which poor Blair tramped all over England. This must have come into his possession," he added, handling the photograph, "without any name or any clue whatever to its situation."

I agreed that we ought to go and see for ourselves, therefore, after spending a quiet evening at the Devonshire, we left by the early train next day for Yorkshire. On arrival at Doncaster station, to which we ran through from London without a stop, we took a fly and drove out upon the broad, snowy highroad through Bentley for about six miles or so, until, after skirting Owston Park we came suddenly upon the crossroads where stood the lonely old house, just as shown in the photograph.

It was a quaint, old place, like one of those old toll-houses one sees in ancient prints, the old bar being of course missing. The gate-post, however, still remained, and snow having fallen in the night the scene presented was truly wintry and picturesque. The antique house with its broad, smoking chimney at the end had apparently been added to since the photograph had been taken, for at right angles was a new wing of red brick, converting it into quite a comfortable abode. Yet, as we approached, the old place rising out of the white, snow-covered plain breathed mutely of those forgotten days when the York and London coaches passed it, when masked gentlemen-of-the-road lurked in these dark, fir plantations which stood out beyond the open common at Kirkhouse Green, and when the post-boys were never tired of singing the praises of those wonderful cheeses at the old *Bell* in Stilton.

Our driver passed the place and about a quarter of a mile further on we stopped him, alighted and walked back together, ordering the man to await us.

On knocking at the door an aged old woman in cap and ribbons, opened it, whereupon Reggie, who assumed the position of spokesman, made excuse that we were passing, and, noticing by its exterior that the place was evidently an old toll-house, could not resist the inducement to call and request to be allowed to look within.

"I'm sure you're very welcome, gentlemen," answered the woman, in her broad, Yorkshire dialect. "It's an old place and lots o' folk have been here and looked over it in my time."

Across the room were the black old beams of two centuries before, the old chimney-corner looked warm and cosy with its oaken, well-polished settle, and the big pot simmering upon the fire. The furniture, too, was little changed since the old coaching days, while about the place was a general air of affluence and comfort.

"You've lived here a long time, I suppose?" Reggie inquired, when we had glanced around and noted the little lancet window in the chimney-corner whence the toll-keeper in the old days could obtain a view for miles along the highroad that ran away across the open moorlands.

"I've been here this three-and-twenty years come next Michaelmas."

"And your husband?"

"Oh! he's here," she laughed, then called, "Come here, Henry, where are you?" and then she added, "He's never left here once since he came home from sea eighteen years ago. We're both so very attached to the old place. A bit lonely, folks would call it, but Burghwallis is only a mile away."

At mention of her husband's return from sea we both pricked up our ears. Here was evidently the man for whom Burton Blair had searched the length and breadth of England.

XIX

Which Contains a Clue

Adoor opened and there came forward a tall, thin, wiry old man with white hair and a pointed grey beard. He had evidently retired on our arrival in order to change his coat, for he wore a blue reefer jacket which had had but little wear, but the collar of which was twisted, showing that he had only that moment assumed it.

His face was deeply wrinkled with long, straight furrows across the brows; the countenance of a man who for years had been exposed to rigours of wind and weather in varying climates.

Having welcomed us, he laughed lightly when we explained our admiration for old houses. We were Londoners, we explained, and toll-houses and their associations with the antiquated locomotion of the past always charmed us.

"Yes," he said, in a rather refined voice for such a rough exterior, "they were exciting days, those. Nowadays the motor car has taken the place of the picturesque coach and team, and they rush past here backwards and forwards, blowing their horns at every hour of the day and night. Half the time we have a constable lying in wait in the back garden ready to time them on to Campsall, and take 'em to the Petty Sessions afterwards!" he laughed; "and fancy this at the very spot where Claude Duval held up the Duke of Northumberland and afterwards gallantly escorted Lady Mary Percy back to Selby."

The old fellow seemed to deplore the passing of the good old days, for he was one of what is known as "the old school," full of narrow-minded prejudices against every new-fangled idea, whether it be in medicine, religion or politics, and declaring that when he was a youth men were men and could hold their own successfully against the foreigner, either in the peace of commerce or in the clash of arms.

To my utter surprise he told us that his name was Hales—the same as that of Mabel's secret lover, and as we chatted with him we learned that he had been a good many years at sea, mostly in the Atlantic and Mediterranean trades.

"Well, you seem pretty comfortable now," I remarked, smiling, "a cosy house, a good wife, and everything to make you happy."

"You're right," he answered, taking down a long clay pipe from the rack over the open hearth. "A man wants nowt more. I'm contented enough and I only wish everybody in Yorkshire was as comfortable this hard weather."

The aged pair seemed flattered at receiving us as visitors, and good-naturedly offered us a glass of ale.

"It's home-brewed, you know," declared Mrs. Hales. "The likes of us can't afford wine. Just taste it," she urged, and being thus pressed we were glad of an excuse to extend our visit.

The old lady had bustled out to the kitchen to fetch glasses, when Reggie rose to his feet, closed the door quickly, and, turning to Hales, said in a low voice—

"We want to have five minutes' private conversation with you, Mr. Hales. Do you recognise this?" and he drew forth the photograph and held it before the old man's eyes.

"Why, it's a picture o' my house," he exclaimed in surprise. "But what's the matter!"

"Nothing, only just answer my questions. They are most important, and our real object in coming here is to put them to you. First, have you ever known a man named Blair—Burton Blair."

"Burton Blair!" echoed the old fellow, his hands on the arms of his chair as he leaned forward intently. "Yes, why?"

"He discovered a secret, didn't he?"

"Yes, through me—made millions out of it, they say."

"When did you last see him?"

"About five or six years ago."

"When he discovered you living here?"

"That's it. He searched every road in England to find me."

"You gave him this photograph?"

"No, I think he stole it."

"Where did you first meet him?"

"On board the *Mary Crowle* in the port of Antwerp. He was at sea, like myself. But why do you wish to know all this?"

"Because," answered Reggie, "Burton Blair is dead, and his secret has been bequeathed to my friend here, Mr. Gilbert Greenwood."

"Burton Blair dead!" cried the old man, jumping to his feet as though he had received a shock. "Burton dead! Does Dicky Dawson know this?"

"Yes, and he is in London," I replied.

"Ah!" he exclaimed, with impatience, as though the premature knowledge held by the man Dawson had upset all his plans. "Who told him? How the devil did he know?"

I had to confess ignorance, but in reply to his demand I deplored the tragic suddenness of our friend's decease, and how I had been left in possession of the pack of cards upon which the cipher had been written.

"Have you any idea what his secret really was?" asked the wiry old fellow. "I mean of where his great wealth came from?"

"None whatever," was my reply. "Perhaps you can tell us something?"

"No," he snapped, "I can't. He became suddenly rich, although only a month or so before he was on tramp and starving. He found me and I gave him certain information for which I was afterwards well repaid. It was this information, he told me, which formed the key to the secret."

"Was it anything to do with this pack of cards and the cipher?" I inquired eagerly.

"I don't know, I've never seen the cards you mention. When he arrived here one cold night, he was exhausted and starving and dead beat. I gave him a meal and a bed, and told him what he wanted to know. Next morning, with money borrowed from me, he took train to London and the next I heard of him was a letter which stated that he had paid into the County Bank at York to my credit one thousand pounds, as we had arranged to be the price of the information. And I tell you, gentlemen, nobody was more surprised than I was to receive a letter from the bank next day, confirming it. He afterwards deposited a similar sum in the bank, on the first of January every year—as a little present, he said."

"Then you never saw him after the night that his search for you was successful?"

"No, not once," Hales answered, addressing his wife, who had just entered, saying that he was engaged in a private conversation, and requesting her to leave us, which she did. "Burton Blair was a queer character," Hales continued, addressing me, "he always was. No better sailor ever ate salt junk. He was absolutely fearless and a splendid navigator. He knew the Mediterranean as other men know Cable Street, Whitechapel, and had led a life cram-full of adventure. But he was a reckless devil ashore—very reckless. I remember once how we both narrowly escaped with our lives at a little town outside Algiers. He pulled an Arab girl's veil off her face out of sheer mischief, and, when she raised the alarm, we had to make ourselves scarce, pretty

WILLIAM LE QUEUX

quick, I can tell you," and he laughed heartily at the recollection of certain sprees ashore. "But both he and I had had pretty tough times in the Cameroons and in the Andes. I was older than he, and when I first met him I laughed at what I believed to be his ignorance. But I soon saw that he'd crammed about double the amount of travelling and adventure into his short spell than ever I had done, for he had a happy knack of deserting and going up country whenever an opportunity offered. He'd fought in half-a-dozen revolutions in Central and South America and used to declare that the rebels in Guatemala, had, on one occasion, elected him Minister of Commerce!"

"Yes," I agreed, "he was in many ways a most remarkable man with a most remarkable history His life was a mystery from beginning to end, and it is that mystery which now, after his death, I am trying to unravel."

"Ah! I fear you'll find it a very difficult task," replied his old friend, shaking his head. "Blair was secret in everything. He never let his right hand know what his left did. You could never get at the bottom of his ingenuity, or at his motives. And," he added, as though it were an afterthought, "can you assign any reason why he should have left his secret in your hands?"

"Well, only gratitude," I replied. "I was able on one occasion to render him a little assistance."

"I know. He told me all about it—how you had both put his girl to school, and all that. But," he went on, "Blair had some motive when he left you that unintelligible cipher, depend upon it. He knew well enough that you would never obtain its solution alone."

"Why?"

"Because others had tried before you and failed."

"Who are they?" I inquired, much surprised.

"Dick Dawson is one. If he had succeeded he might have stood in Blair's shoes—a millionaire. Only he wasn't quite cute enough, and the secret passed on to your friend."

"Then you don't anticipate that I shall ever discover the solution of the cipher?"

"No," answered the old man, very frankly, "I don't. But what of his girl—Mabel, I think she was called?"

"She's in London and has inherited everything," I replied; whereat the old fellow's furrowed face broadened into a grim smile, and he remarked—

"A fine catch for some young fellow, she'd make. Ah! if you could induce her to tell all she knows she could place you in possession of her father's secret."

"Does she actually know it?" I cried quickly. "Are you certain of this?"

"I am; she knows the truth. Ask her."

"I will," I declared. "But cannot you tell us the nature of the information you gave to Blair on that night when he re-discovered you?" I asked persuasively.

"No," he replied in a decisive tone, "it was a confidential matter and must remain as such. I was paid for my services, and as far as I am concerned, I have wiped my hands of the affair."

"But you could tell me something concerning this strange quest of Blair's—something, I mean, that might put me on the track of the solution of the secret."

"The secret of how he gained his wealth, you mean, eh?"

"Of course."

"Ah, my dear sir, you'll never discover that—mark me—if you live to be a hundred. Burton Blair took jolly good care to hide that from everybody."

"And he was well assisted by such men as your self," I said, rather impertinently, I fear.

"Perhaps, perhaps so," he said quickly, his face flushing. "I promised him secrecy and I've kept my promise, for I owe my present comfortable circumstances solely to his generosity."

"A millionaire can do anything, of course. His money secures him his friends."

"Friends, yes," replied the old man, gravely; "but not happiness. Poor Burton Blair was one of the unhappiest of men, that I am quite certain of."

He spoke the truth, I knew. The millionaire had himself many times declared to me in confidence that he had been far happier in his days of penury and careless adventure beyond the seas, than as possessor of that great West End mansion, and the first estate in Herefordshire.

"Look here," exclaimed Hales, suddenly, glancing keenly from Reggie to myself, "I give you warning," and he dropped his voice to almost a whisper. "You say that Dick Dawson has returned—beware of him. He means mischief, you may bet your hat on that! Be very careful of his girl, too, she knows more than you think."

"We have a faint suspicion that Blair did not die a natural death," I remarked.

"You have?" he exclaimed, starting. "What causes you to anticipate that?"

"The circumstances were so remarkable," I replied, and continuing, I explained the tragic affair just as I have written it here.

"You don't suspect Dicky Dawson, I suppose?" the old fellow asked anxiously.

"Why? Had he any motive for getting rid of our friend?"

"Ah! I don't know. Dicky is a very funny customer. He always held Blair beneath his thumb. They were a truly remarkable pair; the one blossoming forth into a millionaire, and the other living strictly in secret somewhere abroad—in Italy, I think."

"Dawson must have had some very strong motive for remaining so quiet," I observed.

"Because he was compelled," answered Hales, with a mysterious shake of the head. "There were reasons why he shouldn't show his face. Myself, I wonder why he has dared to do so now."

"What!" I cried eagerly, "is he wanted by the police or something?"

"Well," answered the old man, after some hesitation, "I don't think he'd welcome a visit from any of those inquisitive gentlemen from Scotland Yard. Only remember I make no charges, none at all. If, however, he attempts any sharp practice, you may just casually mention that Harry Hales is still alive, and is thinking of coming up to London to pay him a morning call. Just watch what effect those words will have upon him," and the old man chuckled to himself, adding, "Ah! Mr. Dicky-bird Dawson, you've got to reckon with me yet, I fancy."

"Then you'll assist us?" I cried in eagerness. "You can save Mabel Blair if you will?"

"I'll do all I can," was Hales' outspoken reply, "for I recognise that there's some very ingenious conspiracy afoot somewhere." Then, after a long pause, during which he had re-filled his long clay, and his eyes fixed thoughtfully upon mine, the old man added, "You told me a little while ago that Blair had left you his secret, but you didn't explain to me the exact terms of his will. Was anything said about it?"

"In the clause which bequeaths it to me is a strange rhyme which runs—

"King Henry the Eighth was a knave to his queens.
He'd one short of seven—and nine or ten scenes!'

"and he also urged me to preserve the secret from every man as he had done. But," I added bitterly, "the secret being in cipher I cannot obtain knowledge of it."

"And have you no key?" smiled the hard-faced old seafarer in the thick reefer.

"None—unless," and at that moment a strange thought flashed for the first time upon me, "unless the key is actually concealed within that rhyme!" I repeated the couplet aloud. Yes, all the cards of that piquet pack were mentioned in it—king, eight, knave, queen, seven, nine, ten!

My heart leapt within me. Could it be possible that by arranging the cards in the following order the record could be read?

If so, then Burton Blair's strange secret was mine at last!

I mentioned my sudden and startling theory, when the tall old fellow's grey face broadened into a triumphant grin and he said—

"Arrange the cards and try it."

XX

The Reading of the Record

The envelope containing the thirty-two cards reposed in my pocket, together with the linen-mounted photograph, therefore, clearing the square old oak table, I opened them out eagerly, while Reggie and the old man watched me breathlessly.

"The first mentioned in the rhyme is king," I said. "Let us have all four kings together."

Having arranged them, I placed the four eights, the four knaves, the queens, aces, sevens, nines and tens, in the order given by the doggerel.

Reggie was quicker than I was in reading down the first column and declared it to be a hopeless jumble entirely unintelligible. I read for myself, and, deeply disappointed, was compelled to admit that the key was not, after all, to be found there.

Yet I recollected what my friend in Leicester had explained, how the record would be found in the first letter on each card being read consecutively from one to another through the whole pack, and tried over and over again to arrange them in intelligible order, but without any success. The cipher was just as tantalising and bewildering as it had ever been.

Whole nights I had spent with Reggie, trying in vain to make something of it, but failing always, unable to make out one single word.

I transcribed the letters backwards, but the result upon my piece of paper was the same.

"No," remarked old Hales, "you haven't got hold of it yet. I'm sure, however, you are near it. That rhyme gives the key—you mark me."

"I honestly believe it does if we could only discover the proper arrangement," I declared in breathless excitement.

"That's just it," remarked Reggie, in dismay. "That's just where the ingenuity of the cipher lies. It's so very simple, and yet so extraordinarily complicated that the possible combinations run into millions. Think of it!"

"But we have the rhyme which distinctly shows their arrangement:—

> "*King Henry the Eighth was a knave to his queen,*
> *He'd one short of seven and nine or ten—*'

"That's plain enough, and we ought, of course, to have seen it from the first," I said.

"Well, try the king of one suit, the eight of another, the knave of another—and so on," Hales suggested, bending with keen interest over the faces of the pigmy cards.

Without loss of time I took his advice, and carefully relaid the cards in the manner he suggested. But again the result was an unintelligible array of letters, puzzling, baffling and disappointing.

I recollected what my expert friend had told me, and my heart sank.

"Don't you really know now the means by which the problem can be solved?" I asked of old Mr. Hales, being seized with suspicion that he was well aware of it.

"I'm sure I can't tell you," was his quick response. "To me, however, it seems certain that the rhyme in some way forms the key. Try another assortment."

"Which? What other can I try?" I asked blankly, but he only shook his head.

Reggie, with paper and pencil, was trying to make the letters intelligible by the means I had several times tried—namely, by substituting A for B, C for D, and so on. Then he tried two letters added, three letters added, and more still, in order to discover some key, but, like myself, he was utterly foiled.

Meanwhile, the old man who seemed to be fingering the cards with increased interest was, I saw, trying to rearrange them himself by placing his finger upon one and then another, and then a third, as though he knew the proper arrangement, and was reading the record to himself.

Was it possible that he actually held the key to what we had displayed, and was learning Burton Blair's secret while we remained in ignorance of it!

Of a sudden, the wiry old seafarer straightened his back, and, looking at me, exclaimed, with a triumphant smile—

"Now, look here, Mr. Greenwood, there are four suites, aren't there? Try them in alphabetical order—that would be clubs, diamonds, hearts and spades. First take all the clubs and arrange them king, eight, knave, queen, ace, seven, nine, ten, then the diamonds, and afterwards the other two suites. Then see what you make of it."

Assisted by Reggie, I proceeded to again resort the cards into suites, and to arrange them according to the rhyme in four columns of eight each upon the table, the suites as he suggested, in alphabetical order.

"At last!" shouted Reggie, almost beside himself with joy. "At last! Why, we've got it, old chap! Look! Read the first letter on each card straight down, one after the other? What do you make it spell?"

All three of us were breathless—old Hales apparently the most excited of all—or perhaps, he had been misleading us and pretending ignorance.

I had, as yet, only placed the first suite, the clubs, but they read as follows:—

King.	B O N T D R N N C R O A U I T
Eight.	E I T Y G O J T A E N N W N H
Knave.	T N H J E N T Y N D J O I D E
Queen.	W T E S J T H F D T O L L T C
Ace.	E W J I W H E O E H N D L H R
Seven.	E H L X H E F U F E E E F E O
Nine.	N E E P E F I R E R W O I O S
Ten.	T R F A R I F J N E I N N L S

"Why!" I cried, staring at the first intelligible word I had discovered. "The first column commences 'Between.'"

"Yes, and I see other words in the other columns!" cried Reggie, excitedly snatching some of the cards from me in his excitement, and assisting me to rearrange the other suites.

Those moments were among the most breathless and exciting of my life. The great secret which had brought Burton Blair all his fabulous wealth was about to be revealed to us.

It might render me a millionaire as it had already done its dead possessor!

At last the cards being all arranged in their proper order, the eight diamonds, eight hearts and eight spades beneath the eight clubs, I took a pencil and wrote down the first letter on each card.

"Yes!" I cried, almost beside myself with excitement, "the arrangement is perfect. Blair's secret is revealed!"

"Why, it's some kind of record!" exclaimed Reggie. "And it begins with the words 'Between the Ponte del Diavolo!' That's Italian for the Devil's Bridge, I suppose!"

"The Ponte del Diavolo is an old mediaeval bridge near Lucca," I explained quickly, and then I recollected the grave-faced Capuchin, who lived in that silent monastery close by. But at that moment all my attention was given to the transcript of the cipher, and I had no time for reflection. The letter "J" was inserted sometimes in place of a space, apparently in order to throw the lettering out, and so conceal it from any chance solution.

At length, after nearly a quarter of an hour, for certain of the faded letters on the cards were almost obliterated, I discovered that the decipher I had scribbled was a strange record as follows:—"Between the Ponte del Diavolo and the point where the Serchio joins the Lima on the left bank, four hundred and fifty-six paces from the foot of the bridge, where the sun shines only one hour on the fifth of April and two hours on the fifth of May, at noon, descend twenty-four foot-holes behind where a man can defend himself against four hundred. There two big rocks one on each side. On one will be found cut the figure of an old 'E.' On the right hand go down and you will find what you seek. But first find the old man who lives at the crossways."

"I wonder what it all means!" remarked Reggie, who, turning to old Mr. Hales, added, "The latter indicates you," whereat the old fellow laughed knowingly, and we saw that he knew more of Blair's affairs than he would admit.

"It means," I said, "that some secret is concealed in that narrow, romantic valley of the Serchio, and these are the directions for its discovery. I know the winding river where through ages the water has cut deeply down into a rocky bed full of giant boulders and wild leaping torrents and deep pools. Of the pointed Ponte del Diavolo are told many quaint stories of the devil building the bridge and taking for his own the first living thing to pass over it, which proved to be a dog. Indeed," I added, "the spot is one of the wildest and most romantic in all rural Tuscany. Strange, too, the Fra Antonio should live in the monastery only three miles from the spot indicated."

"Who is Fra Antonio?" asked Hales, still gazing upon the cards thoughtfully.

I explained, whereupon the old fellow smiled, and I felt certain that he recognised in the monk's description one of Blair's friends of days bygone.

"Who actually wrote this record?" I inquired of him. "It was not Blair, that's plain."

WILLIAM LE QUEUX

"No," was his reply. "Now that it has been legally left to you by our friend, and that you have succeeded in deciphering it, I may as well tell you something more concerning it."

"Yes, do," we both cried eagerly with one breath.

"Well, it happened in this way," explained the thin old fellow, pressing down the tobacco hard into his long clay. "Some years ago I was serving as first mate on the barque *Annie Curtis* of Liverpool, engaged in the Mediterranean fruit trade and running regularly between Naples, Smyrna, Barcelona, Algiers and Liverpool. Our crew was a mixed one of English, Spaniards and Italians, and among the latter was an old fellow named Bruno. He was a mysterious individual from Calabria, and among the crew it was whispered that he had once been the head of a noted band of brigands who had terrorised that most southern portion of Italy, and who had only recently been exterminated by the Carabineers. The other Italians nicknamed him Baffitone, which in their language is, I believe, Big Moustache. He was a hard worker, drank next to nothing, and was apparently rather well-educated, for he spoke and wrote English quite well, and further he was always worrying everybody to devise ciphers, the solution of which he would set himself in his leisure to puzzle out. One day, on a religious feast, made excuse by the Italians for a holiday, I found him in the forecastle writing something on a small pack of cards. He tried to conceal what he was doing, but, my curiosity aroused, I detected at once how he had arranged them, and the very fact told me what a remarkably ingenious cipher he had discovered."

The old man paused for a moment, as though he hesitated to tell us the whole truth. Presently when he had lit his pipe with a spill, he resumed, saying—

"I left the sea, came back to my wife here, and for fully six years saw nothing of the Italian until one day, looking well and prosperous in a suit of brand new clothes and a new hard hat, he called upon me. He was still on the *Annie Curtis*, but she was in dry dock, and therefore he was, he said, having a bit of a spree ashore. He remained here with me for two days, and with his little camera, evidently a fresh acquisition he snapshotted every conceivable object, including this house. Before he went away he took me into his confidence and told me that what had been suspected of him on board the *Annie Curtis* was true, that he was none other than the notorious Poldo Pensi, the brigand whose daring and ferocity had long been chronicled in Italian song and story. He had, however, since the breaking up of his band, become a reformed character, and rather than profit by certain knowledge that he had obtained while an outlaw, he worked for his living on board an English ship. The knowledge, he said, was obtained from a certain Cardinal Sannini of the Vatican whom he had held to ransom, and was of such a character that he might become a rich man any day he wished, but having regard to the fact that the Government had offered a large reward for his capture either dead or alive, he deemed it best to conceal his identity and sail the seas. But he told me, here in this room, as we sat smoking together the night before he departed, that the secret was on record, but in such a manner that any one discovering it would not be able to read it without possessing the key to the cipher."

"Then he left it on these cards!" I cried, interrupting.

"Exactly. The secret of Cardinal Sannini, obtained by the notorious outlaw Poldo Pensi, whose terrible band ravaged half Italy twenty-five years ago, and who compelled Pope Pius IX himself to pay tribute to them, is written here—just as you have deciphered it."

"Is this man Pensi dead?" I inquired.

"Oh yes, he died and was buried at sea, somewhere off Lisbon, before Burton Blair came into possession of the cards. The secret, I ascertained, was wrung from Cardinal Sannini, who, while on his way across the wild, inhospitable country between Reggio and Gerace was seized by Pensi and his gang, taken up to their stronghold—a small mountain village about three miles from Nicastro—and there held prisoner, a large ransom being about to be demanded of the Holy See. For certain reasons, it seemed, the wily old Cardinal in question did not desire that the Vatican should be made aware of his capture, therefore he made it a condition of his release that he should reveal a certain very remarkable secret—the secret written upon the cards—which he did, and in exchange for which Pensi released him."

"But Sannini was one of the highest placed Cardinals in Rome," I exclaimed. "Why, at the death of Pio Nono, he was believed to be designed as his successor to the Pontificate."

"True," remarked the old man, who seemed well versed in all the recent history of St. Peter's at Rome. "The secret divulged by the Cardinal is undoubtedly one of very great value, and he did so in order to save his own reputation, I believe, for from what the outlaw told me, they had discovered that he was in the extreme south in direct opposition to the Pope's orders, and in order to stir up some religious ill-feeling against Pio Nono. Hence Sannini, so trusted by His Holiness, was compelled at all hazards to keep the facts of his capture an absolute secret. Pensi related how, before releasing the Cardinal, he went himself in secret to a certain spot in Tuscany, and ascertained that what the great ecclesiastic had divulged was absolutely the truth. He was then released, and given safe escort back to Cosenza, whence he took train back to Rome."

"But how came Burton Blair possessed of the secret?" I inquired eagerly.

"Ah!" remarked the old fellow, showing the palms of his hard brown hands, "that's the question. I know that upon these very cards, Poldo Pensi, the ex-brigand of Calabria, inscribed the Cardinal's directions in English. Indeed you will note that the wording betrays a foreigner. Those faded capital letters were traced by him on board the *Annie Curtis*, and he certainly held the secret safely until his death. What he told me I never divulged until—well, until I was compelled to by Burton Blair on that night when he recognised this house from Poldo's photograph, and rediscovered me."

"Compelled you!" Reggie exclaimed. "How?"

XXI

"Worse than Death"

The tall old fellow looked at me with his grey eyes and shook his head.

"Burton Blair knew rather too much," he answered evasively. "He had, it seemed, been raised to chief mate of the *Annie Curtis*, when I left her, and Poldo, the man who had held dukes and cardinals and other great men to ransom, worked patiently under him. Then after a bad go of fever Poldo died, and strangely enough gave—so Blair declared—the pack of cards with the secret into his hands. Dicky Dawson, however, who was also on board as bo'sun, and who had lived half his life on Italian brigs in the Adriatic, declares that this story is untrue, and that Blair stole the little bag containing the cards from beneath Poldo's pillow half an hour before he died. That, however, may be the truth, or a lie, yet the facts remain, that Poldo must have let out some portion of his secret in the delirium of the fever and that the little cards passed into Blair's possession. Three weeks after the Italian's death, Blair, on landing at Liverpool, carrying with him the cards and the snap-shot photograph, set out on that very long and fatiguing journey up and down all the roads in England, in order to find me, and learn from me the key to the secret of the outlaws which I held."

"And when at last he found you, what then?"

"He alleged solemnly that Bruno had given it to him as a dying gift, and that his reason for seeking me was because the old outlaw had, before he died, requested to see the photograph from his sea-chest, and looking upon it for a long time, had said to himself reflectively in Italian, 'There lives in that house the only man who knows my secret.' For that reason Blair evidently secured the picture after the Italian's death. On arrival here he showed me the cards, and promised me a thousand pounds if I would reveal the Italian's confidences. As the man was dead, I saw no reason to withhold them, and in exchange for a promise to pay the amount I told him what he wanted to know, and among other matters explained the rearrangement of the cards, so that he could decipher them. The key to the cipher I had learnt on that festival when I had discovered Poldo writing upon a pack of cards a message, evidently intended for the

Cardinal himself at Rome, for I have since established the fact that the outlaw and the ecclesiastic were in frequent but secret communication prior to the latter's death."

"But this man Dawson must have profited enormously by the revelation made by Blair," I remarked. "They seem to have been most intimate friends."

"Of course he profited," Hales replied. "Blair, possessing this remarkable secret, went in deadly fear of Dicky, the bo'sun, who might declare, as he had already done, that he had stolen it from the dying man. He was well aware that Dawson was an unscrupulous sailor of the very worst type, therefore he considered it a very judicious course, I suppose, to go into partnership with him and assist in the exploration of the secret. But poor Blair must have been in the fellow's hands all through although it is plain that the gains Blair made were enormous, while those of Dicky have been equal, although it seems probable that the latter has lived in absolute obscurity."

"Dawson feared to come to England," Reggie remarked.

"Yes," answered the old man. "There was a rather ugly incident in Liverpool a few years ago—that's the reason."

"There is no negative evidence regarding the actual gift of the pack of cards to Blair by this reformed outlaw, is there!" I inquired.

"None whatever. For my own part I believe that Poldo gave them to Blair together with instruction to return ashore and find me, because he had showed him many little kindnesses during repeated illnesses. Poldo, on giving up his evil ways, had become religious and used to attend sailors' Bethels and missions when ashore, while Blair was, as you know, a very God-fearing man for a sailor. When I recollect all the circumstances, I believe it was only natural that Poldo should give the dead Cardinal's secret into the hands of his best friend."

"The spot indicated is near Lucca in Tuscany," I remarked. "You say that this outlaw, Poldo Pensi, had been there and made an investigation. What did he find?"

"He found what the Cardinal had told him he would find. But he never explained to me its nature. All he would tell was that the secret would render its possessor a very wealthy man—which it certainly did in Blair's case."

"The connexion of the Church between the late Cardinal Sannini and Fra Antonio, the Monk of Lucca, is strange," I observed. "Is the monk, I wonder, in possession of the secret? He certainly had some connexion with the affair, as shown by his constant consultations with the man Dawson."

"No doubt," remarked Reggie, turning over the little cards idly. "We've now got to discover the exact position of both men, and at the same time prevent this fellow Dawson from obtaining too firm a hold on Mabel Blair's fortune."

"Leave that to me," I said confidently. "For the present our line of action is quite clear. We must investigate the spot on the bank of the Serchio and discover what is hidden there." Then turning to Hales, I added, "In the record it is, I notice, distinctly directed 'First find the old man who lives at the house by the crossways.' What does that mean? Why is that direction given?"

"Because I suppose that when the record was written upon these cards I was the only other person having any knowledge of the Cardinal's secret—the only person, too, possessing the key to the cipher."

"But you affected ignorance of all this at first," I said, still viewing the old fellow with some suspicion.

"Because I was not certain of your *bona-fides*," he laughed quite frankly. "You took me by surprise, and I was not inclined to show my hand prematurely."

"Then you have really told us all you know?" Reggie said.

"Yes, I know no more," he replied. "As to what is contained at the spot indicated in the record, I am quite ignorant. Remember that Blair has paid me justly, even more than he stipulated, but as you are well aware he was a most reserved man concerning his own affairs, and left me in entire ignorance."

"You can give us no further information regarding this one-eyed man who seems to have been Blair's partner in the extraordinary enterprise?"

"None, except that he's a very undesirable acquaintance. It was Poldo who nicknamed him 'The Ceco.'"

"And the monk who calls himself Fra Antonio?"

"I know nothing of him—never heard of any such person."

It was upon the tip of my tongue to inquire whether the old man had a son, and if that son's name was Herbert, recollecting, as I did, that tragic midnight scene in Mayvill Park. Yet, fortunately perhaps, I was prompted to remain silent, preferring to conceal my knowledge and to await developments of the extraordinary situation.

Still a fierce, mad jealousy was gnawing at my heart. Mabel, the calm, sweet girl I loved so well, and whose future had been entrusted to me, had, like so many other girls, committed the grievous error of falling in love with a common man, rough, uncouth, and far beneath her station. Love in a cottage—about which we hear so much—is all very well in theory, just as is the empty-pocket-light-heart fallacy, but in these modern days the woman habituated to luxury can never be happy in the four-roomed house any more than the man who gallantly marries for love and foregoes his inheritance.

No. Each time I recollected that young ruffian's sneers and threats, his arrogance and his final outburst of murderous passion, which had been so near producing a fatal termination to my well-beloved, my blood boiled. My anger was aflame. The fellow had escaped, but within myself I determined that he should not go scot-free.

And yet, when I recollected, it seemed as though Mabel were utterly and irresistibly in that man's power, even though she had attempted defiance.

We remained with Hales and his wife for another hour learning few additional facts except from a word that the old lady let drop. I ascertained that they actually had a son whose name was Herbert, but whose character was none too good.

"He was in the stables at Belvoir," his mother explained when I made inquiry of him. "But he left nearly two years ago, and we haven't seen him since. He writes sometimes from various places and appears to be prospering."

The fellow was, therefore, as I had surmised from his appearance, a horsekeeper, a groom, or something of that kind.

It was already half-past seven when we arrived back at King's Cross, and after a hasty chop at a small Italian restaurant opposite the station, we both drove to Grosvenor Square, in order to explain to Mabel our success in the solution of the cipher.

Carter, who admitted us, knew us so well that he conducted us straight upstairs to the great drawing-room, so artistically lit with its shaded electric lights placed cunningly in all sorts of out-of-the-way corners. Upon the table was a great old punch-bowl, full of splendid Gloire de Dijon roses, which the head gardener sent with the fruit from the house at Mayvill daily. Their arrangement was, I knew, by the hand of the woman whom for years I had secretly admired and loved. Upon a side table was a fine panel photograph of poor Burton Blair in a heavy silver frame, and upon the corner his daughter had placed a tiny bow of crape to honour the dead man's memory. The great house was full of those womanly touches that betrayed the sweet sympathy of her character and the calm tranquillity of her life.

Presently the door opened, and we both rose to our feet, but instead of the bright, sunny-hearted girl with the musical voice and merry, open face, there entered the middle-aged bearded man in gold-rimmed glasses, who was once the bo'sun of the barque *Annie Curtis* of Liverpool, and afterwards had been the secret partner of Burton Blair.

"Good evening, gentlemen," he exclaimed, bowing with that forced veneer of polish he sometimes assumed. "I am very pleased to welcome you here in my late friend's house. I have, as you will perceive, taken up my quarters here in accordance with the terms of poor Blair's will, and I am pleased to have this opportunity of again meeting you."

The fellow's cool impudence took us both entirely aback. He seemed so entirely confident that his position was unassailable.

"We called to see Miss Blair," I explained. "We were not aware that you were about to take up your residence here quite so quickly."

"Oh, it is best," he assured us. "There are a great many matters in connexion with Blair's wide interests that require immediate attention," and as he was speaking, the door again opened and there entered a dark-haired woman of about twenty-six, of medium height, rather showily dressed in a black, low-cut gown, but whose countenance was of a rather common type, yet, nevertheless, somewhat prepossessing.

"My daughter, Dolly," explained the one-eyed man. "Allow me to introduce you," and we both gave her rather a cold bow, for it seemed that they had both made their abode there, and taken over the management of the house in their own hands.

"I suppose Mrs. Percival still remains?" I inquired after a few moments, on recovering from the shock at finding the adventurer and his daughter were actually in possession of that splendid mansion which half London admired and the other half envied—the place of which numerous photographs and descriptions had appeared in the magazines and ladies' journals.

"Yes, Mrs. Percival is still in her own sitting-room. I left her there five minutes ago. Mabel, it seems, went out at eleven o'clock this morning and has not returned."

"Not returned," I exclaimed in quick surprise. "Why not?"

"Mrs. Percival seems to be very upset. Fears something has happened to her, I think."

Without another word I ran down the broad staircase with its crystal balustrade and, tapping at the door of the room, set apart for Mrs. Percival, and announcing my identity, was at once allowed admittance.

The instant the prim elderly widow saw me she sprang to her feet in terrible distress, crying—

"Oh, Mr. Greenwood, Mr. Greenwood! What can we do? How can we treat these terrible people? Poor Mabel left this morning and drove in the brougham to Euston Station. There she gave Peters this letter, addressed to you, and then dismissed the carriage. What can it possibly mean?"

I took the note she handed me and tremblingly tore it open, to find a few hurriedly scribbled lines in pencil upon a sheet of notepaper, as follows:—

Dear Mr. Greenwood,

You will no doubt be greatly surprised to learn that I have left home for ever. I am well aware that you entertain for me as high a regard and esteem as I do for you, but as my secret must come out, I cannot remain to face you of all men. These people will hound me to death, therefore I prefer to live in secret beyond the reach of their taunts and their vengeance than to remain and have the finger of scorn pointed at me. My father's secret can never become yours, because his enemies are far too wily and ingenious. Every precaution has been taken to secure it against all your endeavours. Therefore, as your friend I tell you it is no use grinding the wind. All is hopeless! Exposure means to me a fate worse than death! Believe me that only desperation has driven me to this step because my poor father's cowardly enemies and mine have triumphed. Yet at the same time I ask you to forget entirely that any one ever existed of the name of the ill-fated, unhappy and heartbroken Mabel Blair."

I stood with the open, tear-stained letter in my hand absolutely speechless.

XXII

THE MYSTERY OF A NIGHT'S ADVENTURE

E xposure means to me a fate worse than death," she wrote. What could it mean?

Mrs. Percival divined by my face the gravity of the communication, and, rising quickly to her feet, she placed her hand tenderly upon my shoulder, asking—

"What is it, Mr. Greenwood? May I not know?"

For answer I handed her the note. She read it through quickly, then gave vent to a loud cry of dismay, realising that Burton Blair's daughter had actually fled. That she held the man Dawson in fear was plain. She dreaded that her own secret, whatever it was, must now be exposed, and had, it seemed, fled rather than again face me. But why? What could her secret possibly be that she was so ashamed that she was bent upon hiding herself?

Mrs. Percival summoned the coachman, Crump, who had driven his young mistress to Euston, and questioned him.

"Miss Mabel ordered the *coupe* just before eleven, ma'am," the man said, saluting. "She took her crocodile dressing-bag with her, but last night she sent away a big trunk by Carter Patterson—full of old clothing, so she told her maid. I drove her to Euston Station where she alighted and went into the booking-hall. She kept me waiting about five minutes, when she brought a porter who took her bag, and she then gave me the letter addressed to Mr. Greenwood to give to you. I drove home then, ma'am."

"She went to the North, evidently," I remarked when Crump had left and the door had closed behind him. "It looks as though her flight was premeditated. She sent away her things last night."

I was thinking of that arrogant young stable worker, Hales, and wondering if his renewed threats had really caused her to keep another tryst with him. If so, it was exceedingly dangerous.

"We must find her," said Mrs. Percival, resolutely. "Ah!" she sighed, "I really don't know what will happen, for the house is now in possession of this odious man Dawson and his daughter, and the man is a most uncouth, ill-bred fellow. He addresses the servants with an easy familiarity, just as though they were his equals; and just now, he actually complimented one of the housemaids upon her good looks! Terrible, Mr. Greenwood, terrible," exclaimed the widow, greatly shocked. "Most disgraceful show of ill-breeding! I certainly cannot remain here now Mabel has thought fit to leave, without even consulting me. Lady Rainham called this afternoon, but of course I had to be not at home. What can I tell people in these distressing circumstances?"

I saw how scandalised was the estimable old chaperone, for she was nothing if not a straightforward widow, whose very life depended upon rigorous etiquette and the traditions of her honourable family. Cordial and affable to her equals, yet she was most frigid and unbending to all inferiors, cultivating a habit of staring at them through her square eyeglass rimmed with gold, and surveying them as though they were surprising creatures of a different flesh and blood. It was this latter idiosyncrasy which always annoyed Mabel, who held the very womanly creed that one should be kind and pleasant to inferiors and cold only to enemies. Nevertheless, under Mrs. Percival's protective wing and active tuition, Mabel herself had gone into the best circle of society whose doors are ever open to the daughter of the millionaire, and had established a reputation as one of the most charming *debutantes* of her season.

How society has altered in these past ten years! Nowadays, the golden key is the open sesame of the doors of the bluest blood in England.

The old exclusive circles are no longer, or if there are any, they are obscure and dowdy. Ladies go to music halls and glorified night-clubs. What used to be regarded as the drawback from the dinner at a restaurant is now a principal attraction. A gentlewoman a generation ago reasonably objected that she did not know whom she might sit next. Now, as was the case at the theatre in the pre-Garrick days, the loose character of a portion of the visitors constitutes in itself a lure. The more flagrant the scandal concerning some bedizened "impropriety" the greater the inducement to dine in her company, and, if possible, in her vicinity. Of such is the tone and trend of London society to-day!

For a quarter of an hour, while Reggie was engaged with Dawson *pere et fille*, I took counsel with the widow, endeavouring to form some idea of where Mabel had concealed herself. Mrs. Percival's idea was that she would reveal her whereabouts ere long, but, knowing her firmness of character as well as I did, I held a different opinion. Her letter was one of a woman who had made a resolve and meant at all hazards to keep it. She feared to meet me, and for that reason would, no doubt, conceal her identity. She had a separate account at Coutts' in her own name, therefore she would not be compelled to reveal her whereabouts through want of funds.

Ford, the dead man's secretary, a tall, clean-shaven, athletic man of thirty, put his head into the room, but, finding us talking, at once withdrew. Mrs. Percival had already questioned him, she said, but he was entirely unaware of Mabel's destination.

The man Dawson had now usurped Ford's position in the household, and the latter, full of resentment, was on the constant watch and as full of suspicion as we all were.

Reggie rejoined me presently, saying, "That fellow is absolutely a bounder of the very first water. Actually invited me to have a whisky-and-soda—in Blair's house, too! He's treating Mabel's flight as a huge joke, saying that she'll be back quickly enough, and adding that she can't afford to be away long, and that he'll bring her back the very instant he desires her presence here. In fact, the fellow talks just as though she were as wax in his hands, and as if he can do anything he pleases with her."

"He can ruin her financially, that's certain," I remarked, sighing. "But read this, old chap," and I gave him her strangely-worded letter.

"Good Heavens!" he gasped, when he glanced at it, "she's in deadly terror of those people, that's very certain. It's to avoid them and you that she's escaped—to Liverpool and America, perhaps. Remember she's been a great traveller all her youth and therefore knows her way about."

"We must find her, Reggie," I declared decisively.

"But the worst of it is that she's bent on avoiding you," he said. "She has some distinct reason for this, it seems."

"A reason known only to herself," I remarked pensively. "It is surely a *contretemps* that now, just at the moment when we have gained the truth of the Cardinal's secret which brought Blair his fortune, Mabel should voluntarily disappear in this manner. Recollect all we have at stake. We know not who are our friends or who our enemies. We ought both to go out to Italy and discover the spot indicated in that cipher record, or others will probably forestall us, and we may then be too late."

He agreed that the record being bequeathed to me, I ought to take immediate steps to establish my claim to it, whatever might be. We could not disguise from ourselves the fact that Dawson, as Blair's partner and participator of his enormous wealth, must be well aware of the secret, and that he had already, most probably, taken steps to conceal the truth from myself, the rightful owner. He was a power to be reckoned with—a sinister person, possessed of the wiliest cunning and the most devilish ingenuity in the art of subterfuge. Report everywhere gave him that character. He possessed the cold, calm manner of the man who had lived by his wits, and it seemed that in this affair his ingenuity, sharpened by a life of adventure, was to be pitted against my own.

Mabel's sudden resolution and disappearance were maddening. The mystery of her letter, too, was inscrutable. If she were really dreading lest some undesirable fact might be exposed, then she ought to have trusted me sufficiently to take me entirely into her confidence. I loved her, although I had never declared my passion, therefore, ignorant of the truth, she had treated me as I had desired, as a sincere friend. Yet, why had she not sought my aid? Women are such strange creatures, I reflected. Perhaps she loved that fellow after all!

A fevered, anxious week went by and Mabel made no sign. One night I left Reggie at the Devonshire about half-past eleven and walked the damp, foggy London streets until the roar of traffic died away, the cabs crawled and grew infrequent and the damp, muddy pavements were given over to the tramping constable and the shivering outcast. In the thick mist I wandered onward thinking deeply, yet more and more mystified at the remarkable chain of circumstances which seemed hour by hour to become more entangled.

On and on I had wandered, heedless of where my footsteps carried me, passing along Knightsbridge, skirting the Park and Kensington Gardens, and was just passing the corner of the Earl's Court Road when some fortunate circumstance awakened me from my deep reverie, and I became conscious for the first time that I was being followed. Yes, there distinctly was a footstep behind me, hurrying when I hurried, slackening when I slackened. I crossed the road, and, before the long high wall of Holland Park I halted and turned. My pursuer came on a few paces, but drew up suddenly, and I could only distinguish against the glimmer of the street lamp through the London fog a figure long and distorted by the bewildering mist. The latter was not sufficiently dense to prevent me finding my way, for I knew that part of London well. Nevertheless, to be followed so persistently at such an hour was not very pleasant. I was suspicious that some tramp or thief who had passed me by and found me oblivious to my surroundings had turned and followed me with evil intent.

Forward I went again, but as soon as I had done so the light, even tread, almost an echo of my own, came on steadily behind me. I had heard weird stories of madmen who haunt the London streets at night and who follow unsuspecting foot-passengers aimlessly. It is one of the forms of insanity well known to specialists.

Again I recrossed the road, passing through Edwarde's Square and out into Earl's Court Road, thus retracing my steps back towards the High Street, but the mysterious man still followed me so persistently that in the mist, which in that part had grown thicker until it obscured the street lamps, I confess I experienced some uneasiness.

Presently, however, just as I was turning the corner into Lexham Gardens at a point where the fog had obscured everything, I felt a sudden rush, and at the same instant experienced a sharp stinging sensation behind the right shoulder. The shock was such a severe one that I cried out, turning next instant upon my assailant, but so agile was he that, ere I could face him, he had eluded me and escaped.

I heard his receding footsteps—for he was running away down the Earl's Court Road—and shouted for the police. But there was no response. The pain in my shoulder became excruciating. The unknown man had struck me with a knife, and blood was flowing, for I felt it damp and sticky upon my hand.

Again I shouted "Police! Police!" until at last I heard an answering voice in the mist and walked in its direction. After several further shouts I discovered the constable and to him related my strange experience.

He held his bull's eye close to my back and said—

"Yes, there's no doubt, sir, you've been stabbed! What kind of a man was he?"

"I never saw him," was my lame reply. "He always kept at a distance from me and only approached at a point where it was too dark to distinguish his features."

"I've seen no one, except a clergyman whom I met a moment ago passing in Earl's Court Road—at least he wore a broad-brimmed hat like a clergyman. I didn't see his face."

"A clergyman!" I gasped. "Do you think it could have been a Roman Catholic priest?" for my thoughts were at that moment of Fra Antonio, who was evidently the guardian of the Cardinal's secret.

"Ah! I'm sure I couldn't tell. I couldn't see his features. I only noted his hat."

"I feel very faint," I said, as a sickening dizziness crept over me. "I wish you'd get me a cab. I think I had better go straight home to Great Russell Street."

"That's a long way. Hadn't you better go round to the West London Hospital first?" the policeman suggested.

"No," I decided. "I'll go home and call my own doctor."

Then I sat upon a doorstep at the end of Lexham Gardens and waited while the constable went in search of a hansom in the Old Brompton Road.

Had I been attacked by some homicidal maniac who had followed me all that distance, or had I narrowly escaped being the victim of foul assassination? To me the latter theory seemed decidedly the most feasible. There was a strong motive for my death. Blair had bequeathed the great secret to me and I had now learnt the cipher of the cards.

This fact had probably become known to our enemies, and hence their dastardly attempt.

Such a contingency, however, was a startling one, for if it had become known that I had really deciphered the record, then our enemies would most certainly take steps in Italy to prevent us discovering the secret of that spot on the banks of the wild and winding Serchio.

At last the cab came, and, slipping a tip into the constable's palm, I got in, and with my silk muffler placed at my back to staunch the blood, drove slowly on through the fog at little more than foot's-pace.

Almost as soon as I entered the hansom I felt my head swimming and a strange sensation of numbness creeping up my legs. A curious nausea seized me, too, and although I had fortunately been able to stop the flow of blood, which tended to prove that the wound was not such a serious one after all, my hands felt strangely cramped, and in my jaws was a curious pain very much like the commencement of an attack of neuralgia.

I felt terribly ill. The cabman, informed by the constable of my injury, opened the trap-door in the roof to inquire after me, but I could scarcely articulate a reply. If the wound was only a superficial one it certainly had a strange effect upon me.

Of the many misty lights at Hyde Park Corner I have a distinct recollection, but after that my senses seemed bewildered by the fog and the pain I suffered and I recollect nothing more until, when I opened my eyes painfully again, I found myself in my own bed, the daylight shining in at the window and Reggie and our old friend Tom Walker, surgeon, of Queen Anne Street, standing beside me watching me with a serious gravity that struck me at the moment as rather humorous.

Nevertheless, I must admit that there was very little humour in the situation.

XXIII

Which is in Many Ways Amazing

Walker was puzzled, distinctly puzzled. He had, I found, strapped up my wound during my unconsciousness after probing it and injecting various antiseptics, I suppose. He had also called in consultation Sir Charles Hoare, the very distinguished surgeon of Charing Cross Hospital, and both of them had been greatly puzzled over my symptoms.

When, an hour later, I was sufficiently recovered to be able to talk, Walker held my wrist and asked me how it all happened.

After I had explained as well as I could, he said—

"Well, my dear fellow, I can only say you've been about as near to death as any man I've ever attended. It was just a case of touch and go with you. When Seton first called me and I saw you I feared that it was all up. Your wound is quite a small one, superficial really, and yet your collapsed condition has been most extraordinary, and there are certain symptoms so mysterious that they have puzzled both Sir Charles and myself."

"What did the fellow use?"

"Not an ordinary knife, certainly. It was evidently a long, thin-bladed dagger—a stiletto, most probably. I found outside the wound upon the cloth of your overcoat some grease, like animal fat. I am having a portion of it analysed and do you know what I expect to find in it?"

"No; what?"

"Poison," was his reply. "Sir Charles agrees with me in the theory that you were struck with one of those small, antique poignards with perforated blades, used so frequently in Italy in the fifteenth century."

"In Italy!" I cried, the very name of that country arousing within me suspicion of an attempt upon me by Dawson or by his close friend, the Monk of Lucca.

"Yes; Sir Charles, who, as you probably know, possesses a large collection of ancient arms, tells me that in mediaeval Florence they used to impregnate animal fat with some very potent poison and then rub it upon the perforated blade. On striking a victim the act of withdrawing the blade from the wound left a portion of the envenomed grease within, which, of course, produced a fatal effect."

"But you surely don't anticipate that I'm poisoned?" I gasped.

"Certainly you are poisoned. Your wound would neither account for your long insensibility nor for the strange, livid marks upon your body. Look at the backs of your hands!"

I looked as he directed and was horrified to find upon each small, dark, copper-coloured marks, which also covered my wrists and arms.

"Don't be too alarmed, Greenwood," the good-humoured doctor laughed, "you've turned the corner, and you're not going to die yet. You've had a narrow squeak of it, and certainly the weapon with which you were struck was as deadly as any that could be devised, but, fortunately, you had a thick overcoat on, besides other heavy clothing, vests and things, all of which removed the greater part of the venomous substance before it could enter the flesh. And a lucky thing it was for you, I can tell you. Had you been attacked like this in summer, you'd have stood no chance."

"But who did it?" I exclaimed, bewildered, my eyes riveted upon those ugly marks upon my skin, the evidence that some deadly poison was at work within my system.

"Somebody who owed you a very first-class grudge, I should fancy," laughed the surgeon, who had been my friend for many years and who used sometimes to come out hunting with the Fitzwilliams. "But cheer up, old chap, you'll have to live on milk and beef-tea for a day or two, have jour wound dressed and keep very quiet, and you'll soon be bobbing about again."

"That's all very well," I replied, impatiently, "but I've got a host of things to do, some private matters to attend to."

"Then you'll have to let them slide for a day or two, that's very certain."

"Yes," urged Reggie, "you must really keep quiet, Gilbert. I'm only thankful that it isn't so serious as we at first expected. When the cabman brought you home and Glave tore out for Walker, I really thought you'd die before he arrived. I couldn't feel any palpitation of your heart, and you were cold as ice."

"I wonder who was the brute who struck me!" I cried. "Great Jacob! if I'd have caught the fellow, I'd have wrung his precious neck there and then."

"What's the use of worrying, so long as you get better quickly?" Reggie asked philosophically.

But I was silent, reflecting that in the belief of Sir Charles Hoare an old Florentine poison dagger had been used. The very fact caused me to suspect that the dastardly attack had been made upon me by my enemies.

We, of course, told Walker nothing of our curious quest, for the present regarding the affair as strictly confidential. Therefore he treated my injury lightly, declaring that I should quickly recover by the exercise of a little patience.

After he had left, shortly before midday, Reggie sat at my bedside and gravely discussed the situation. The two most pressing points at that moment were first to discover the whereabouts of my well-beloved, and secondly to go out to Italy and investigate the Cardinal's secret.

The days passed, long, weary, gloomy days of early spring, during which I tossed in bed impatient and helpless. I longed to be up and active, but Walker forbade it. He brought me books and papers instead, and enjoined quiet and perfect rest. Although Reggie and I still had our little hunting box down at Helpstone we had not, since Blair's death, been down there. Besides, the season in the lace trade was an unusually busy one, and Reggie now seemed tied to his counting-house more than ever.

So I was left alone the greater part of the day with Glave to attend to my wants, and with one or two male friends who now and then looked in to smoke and chat.

Thus passed the month of March, my progress being much slower than Walker had at first anticipated. On analysis a very dangerous irritant poison had been discovered mixed with the grease, and it appeared that I had absorbed more of it into my system than was at first believed—hence my tardy recovery.

Mrs. Percival, who at our urgent request still remained at Grosvenor Square, visited me sometimes, bringing me fruit and flowers from the hothouses at Mayvill, but she had nothing to report concerning Mabel. The latter had disappeared as completely as though the earth had opened and swallowed her. She was anxious to leave Blair's house now that it was occupied by the usurpers, but we had cajoled her into remaining in order to keep some check upon the movements of the man Dawson and his daughter. Ford had been so exasperated at the man's manner that, on the fifth day of the new *regime*, he had remonstrated, whereupon Dawson had calmly placed a year's wages in banknotes in an envelope, and at once dispensed with his further services, as, of course, he had intended to do all along.

The confidential secretary was, however, assisting us, and at that moment was making every inquiry possible to ascertain the whereabouts of his young mistress.

"The house is absolutely topsy-turvy," declared Mrs. Percival one day, as she sat with me. "The servants are in revolt, and poor Noble, the housekeeper, is having a most terrible time. Carter and eight of the other servants gave notice yesterday. This person Dawson represents the very acme of bad manners and bad breeding, yet I overheard him remarking to his daughter two days ago that he actually contemplated putting up for the Reform and entering Parliament! Ah! what would poor Mabel say, if she knew? The girl, Dolly, as he calls her, the common little wench, has established herself in Mabel's boudoir, and is about to have it re-decorated in daffodil yellow, to suit her complexion, I believe, while as for finances, it seems, from what Mr. Leighton says, that poor Mr. Blair's fortune must go entirely through the fellow's hands."

"It's a shame—an abominable shame!" I cried angrily. "We know that the man is an adventurer, and yet we are utterly powerless," I added bitterly.

"Poor Mabel!" sighed the widow, who was really much devoted to her. "Do you know, Mr. Greenwood," she said, with a sudden air of confidence, "I have thought more than once since her father's death that she is in possession of the truth of the strange connexion between her father and this unscrupulous man who has been given such power over her and hers. Indeed, she has confessed to me as much. And I believe that, if she would but tell us the truth, we might be able to get rid of this terrible incubus. Why doesn't she do it—to save herself?"

"Because she is now in fear of him," I answered in a hard, despairing voice. "She holds some secret of which she lives in terror. That, I believe, accounts for the sudden manner in which she has left her own roof and disappeared. She has left the fellow in undisputed possession of everything."

I had not forgotten Dawson's arrogance and self-confidence on the night he had first called upon us.

"But now, Mr. Greenwood, will you please excuse me for what I am going to say?" asked Mrs. Percival, settling her skirts after a brief pause and looking straight into my face. "Perhaps I have no right to enter into your more private matters in this manner, but I trust you will forgive me when you reflect that I am only speaking on the poor girl's behalf."

"Well!" I inquired, somewhat surprised at her sudden change of manner. Usually she was haughty and frigid in the extreme, a scathing critic who had the names of everybody's cousins aunts and nephews at her fingers' ends.

"The fact is this," she went on. "You might, I feel confident, induce her to tell us the truth. You are the only person who possesses any influence with her now that her father in dead, and—permit me to say so—I have reason for knowing that she entertains a very strong regard for you."

"Yes," I remarked, unable to restrain a sigh, "we are friends—good friends."

"More," declared Mrs. Percival, "Mabel loves you."

"Loves me!" I cried, starting up and supporting myself upon one elbow. "No, I think you must be mistaken. She regards me more as a brother than a lover, and she has, I think, learnt ever since the first day we met in such romantic conditions, to regard me in the light of a protector.

"No," I added, shaking my head, "there are certain barriers that must prevent her loving me—the difference of our ages, of position and all that."

"Ah! There you are entirely mistaken," said the widow, quite frankly. "I happen to know that the very reason why her father left his secret to you was in order that you might profit by its knowledge as he had done, and because he foresaw the direction of Mabel's affections."

"How do you know this, Mrs. Percival?" I demanded, half inclined to doubt her.

"Because Mr. Blair, before making his will, took me into his confidence and asked me frankly whether his daughter had ever mentioned you in such a manner as to cause me to suspect. I told him the truth of course, just as I have now told you. Mabel loves you—loves you very dearly."

"Then for the legacy left me by poor Blair, I am, in a great measure, indebted to you?" I remarked, adding a word of thanks and pondering deeply over the revelation she had just made.

"I only did what was my duty to you both," was her response. "She loves you, as I say, and therefore, by a little persuasion you could, I feel convinced, induce her to tell us the truth concerning this man Dawson. She has fled, it is true, but more in fear of what you may think of her when her secret is out, than of the man himself. Recollect," she added,

"Mabel is passionately fond of you, she has confessed it to me many times, but for some extraordinary reason which remains a mystery, she is endeavouring to repress her affection. She fears, I think, that on your part there is only friendship—that you are too confirmed a bachelor to regard her with any thoughts of affection."

"Oh, Mrs. Percival!" I cried, with a sudden outpouring, "I tell you, I confess to you that I have loved Mabel all along—I love her now, fondly, passionately, with all that fierce ardour that comes to a man only once in his lifetime. She has misjudged me. It is I who have been foolishly at fault, for I have been blind, I have never read her heart's secret."

"Then she must know this at once," was the elderly woman's sympathetic answer. "We must discover her, at all costs, and tell her. There must be a reunion, and she on her part, must confess to you. I know too well how deeply she loves you," she added, "I know how she admires you and how, in the secrecy of her room, she has time after time wept long and bitterly because she believed you were cold and blind to the burning passion of her true pure heart."

But how? The whereabouts of my well-beloved were unknown. She had disappeared completely, in order, it seemed, to escape some terrible revelation which she knew must be made sooner or later.

In the days that followed, while I lay still weak and helpless, both Ford and Reggie were active in their inquiries, but all in vain. I called in the solicitor, Leighton, in consultation, but he could devise no plan other than to advertise, yet to do so was, we agreed, scarcely fair to her.

Curiously enough the dark-faced young woman, Dorothy Dawson, otherwise Dolly, also betrayed the keenest anxiety for Mabel's welfare. Her mother was Italian, and she spoke English with a slight accent, having always, she said, lived in Italy. Indeed, she called upon me once to express her regret at my illness, and I found that she really improved on acquaintance. Her apparent coarseness was only on account of her mixed nationality, and although she was a shrewd young person possessed of all the subtle Italian cunning, Reggie, I think, found her a bright and amusing companion.

All my thoughts were, however, of my sweet lost love, and of that common, arrogant fellow who, by his threats and taunts, held her so irresistibly and secretly in his power.

Why had she fled in terror from me, and why had such a dastardly and ingenious attempt been made to kill me?

I had solved the secret of the cipher only to be plunged still deeper into the mazes of doubt, despair and mystery, for what the closed book of the future held for me, was as you will see, truly startling and bewildering.

The truth when revealed was hard, solid fact, and yet so strange and amazing was it that it staggered all belief.

XXIV

Contains a Terrible Disclosure

M any long and dreary weeks had passed before I had sufficiently recovered to leave the house, and, accompanied by Reggie, take my first drive.

It was mid April, the weather was still cold, and gay London had not yet returned from wintering in Monte Carlo, Cairo or Rome. Each year the society swallows, those people who fly south with the first chill day of autumn, return to town later, and each London season appears to be more protracted than before.

We drove down Piccadilly to Hyde Park Corner, and then, turning along Constitution Hill, drove along the Mall. Here a great desire seized me to rest for a brief while and enjoy the air in St. James's Park; therefore we alighted, paid the cabman, and, leaning upon Reggie's arm, I strolled slowly along the gravelled walks until we found a convenient seat. The glories of St. James's Park, even on an April day, are a joy for ever to the true Londoners. I often wonder that so few people take advantage of them. The wondrous trees, the delicious sheet of water, all the beauties of English rural scenery, and then the sense that all around you are the great palaces and departments, and offices in which the government of our great Empire is carried on—in other words, that commingling of silence at the core of feverish and tumultuous life outside—all these make St. James's Park one of the loveliest retreats in England.

These things Reggie and I repeated to each other, and then, under the soothing influence of the surroundings, there came musings and reminiscences and the long silences which come between friends and are the best symbols of their complete accord of feeling and opinion.

While we were thus seated I became conscious of the fact that we were in the spot above all others where one was certain to see pass, at that time of day most of the prominent political figures of the hour on their way to their various Departments, or to Parliament where the sitting was just commencing. A Cabinet Minister, two Liberal peers, a Conservative whip, and an Under-secretary passed in rapid succession away in the direction of Storey's Gate.

Reggie, who took a great interest in politics, and had often occupied a seat in the Strangers' Gallery, was pointing out to me the politicians who passed, but my thoughts were elsewhere—with my lost love. Now that Mrs. Percival had revealed to me the truth of Mabel's affection I saw how foolish I had been in making pretence of a coldness towards her that was the very opposite to the feeling which really existed in my heart. I had been a fool, and had now to suffer.

During the weeks I had been confined to my room I had obtained a quantity of books, and discovered certain facts concerning the late Cardinal who had divulged the secret—whatever it was—in return for his release. It appeared that Andrea Sannini was a native of Perugia, who became Archbishop of Bologna, and was afterwards given the Cardinal's hat. A great favourite of Pius IX, he was employed by him upon many delicate missions to the various Powers. As a diplomatist he proved himself possessed of remarkable acumen, therefore the Pope appointed him treasurer-general, as well as director of the world-famous museums and galleries of the Vatican. He was, it appeared, one of the most powerful and distinguished figures in the College of Cardinals, and became extremely prominent for the part he played on the occasion of the entry of the Italian troops into the Eternal City in 1870, while on the death of Pius IX, eight years later, he was believed to be designated as his successor, although on election the choice fell upon his colleague, the late Cardinal Pecci, who became Leo XIII.

I was reflecting upon these facts which I had established after a good deal of heavy reading, when Reggie suddenly cried in a low voice,—

"Why, look! there's Dawson's daughter walking with a man!"

I glanced quickly in the direction indicated and saw, crossing the bridge that spanned the lake and approaching in our direction, a well-dressed female figure in a smart jacket of caracul and neat toque, accompanied by a tall thin man in black.

Dolly Dawson was walking at his side leisurely, chatting and laughing, while he ever and anon bent towards her making some remarks. As he raised his head to glance across the water I saw that above his overcoat showed a clerical collar with a tiny piece of Roman purple. The man was evidently a canon or other dignitary of the Catholic Church.

He was about fifty-five, grey-haired, clean-shaven and wore a silk hat of a somewhat ecclesiastical shape, a rather pleasant-looking man in spite of his thin sensitive lips and pale ascetic face.

In an instant it struck me that they had met clandestinely and were sauntering there in order to avoid possible recognition if they walked the streets. The old priest appeared to be treating her with studied politeness, and as I watched him I saw from his slight gesticulations as he spoke that he was no doubt a foreigner.

I pointed out the fact to Reggie, who said—"We must watch them, old chap. They mustn't see us here. I only hope they'll turn off the other way."

For a moment we followed them with our eyes, fearing that, having crossed the bridge, they would turn in our direction, but fortunately they did not, but turned off to the right along the shore of the lake.

"If he really is Italian then he may have come specially from Italy to have an interview with her," I remarked. For ever since I had met the monk, Antonio, there had seemed some curious connexion between the secret of the dead cardinal and the Church of Rome.

"We must try and find out," declared Reggie. "You mustn't remain here. It's getting too cold for you," he added, springing to his feet. "I'll follow them while you return home."

"No," I said. "I'll walk with you for a bit. I'm interested in the little game," and, rising also, I linked my arm in his and went forward by the aid of my stick.

They were walking side by side in earnest conversation. I could tell by the priest's quick gesticulations, the way in which he first waved his closed fingers and then raised his open hand and touched his left forearm, that he was speaking of some secret and the possessor of it who had disappeared. If one knows the Italian well, one can follow in a sense the topic of conversation by the gestures, each one having its particular signification.

Hurrying as well as I could we gradually gained upon them, for presently they slackened their pace, while the priest spoke earnestly, as though persuading the daughter of the ex-boatswain of the *Annie Curtis* to act in some way he was directing.

She seemed silent, thoughtful and undecided. Once she shrugged her shoulders, and half-turned from him as though in defiance, when in a moment the wily cleric became all smiles and apologies. They were talking in Italian without a doubt, so as passers-by might not understand their conversation. His clothes, too, I noticed were of a distinctly foreign cut and he wore low shoes, the bright steel buckles of which he had evidently taken off.

As they had come across the bridge she had been laughing merrily at some quaint remark of her companion's, but now it appeared as though all her gaiety had died out and she had realised the true object of the stranger's mission. The path they had taken led straight across to the Horse Guards' Parade, and feeling a few moments later that my weakness would not allow me to walk farther, I was compelled to turn back towards the York Column steps, leaving Reggie to make what observations he could.

I returned home thoroughly exhausted and very cold. Even my big frieze overcoat, which I used for driving when down at Helpstone, did not keep out the biting wind. So I sat over the fire for fully a couple of hours until my friend at last returned.

"I've followed them everywhere," he explained, throwing himself into an armchair opposite me. "He's evidently threatening her, and she is afraid of him When they got to the Horse Guards they turned back along Birdcage Walk and then across the Green Park. Afterwards he drove her in a cab to one of Fuller's shops in Regent Street. The old priest seems mortally afraid of being recognised. Before he left the Green Park he turned up the collar of his overcoat so as to hide that piece of purple at his collar."

"Did you discover his name?"

"I followed him to the *Savoy*, where he is staying. He has given his name as Monsignore Galli, of Rimini."

There our information ended. It, however, was sufficient to show that the ecclesiastic was in London with some distinct purpose, probably to induce the Ceco's daughter to give him certain information which he earnestly desired, and which he intended to obtain by reason of certain knowledge which he possessed.

The days passed with gloom and rain, and Bloomsbury presented its most cheerless aspect. No trace could I discover of my lost love, and no further fact concerning the white-haired monsignore. The latter had, it appeared, left the *Savoy* on the following evening, returning, in all probability, to the Continent, but whether successful in his mission or no we were in complete ignorance.

Dolly Dawson, with whom Reggie had struck up a kind of pleasant friendship, more for the purpose of being able to observe and question her than anything else, called upon us on the day following to inquire after me and hear whether we had learnt anything regarding Mabel's whereabouts. Her father, she told us, was absent from London for a few days, and she was about to leave for Brighton in order to visit an aunt.

Was it possible that Dawson, having learned of my solution of the cipher, had returned to Italy in order to secure the Cardinal's secret from us? I longed hour by hour for strength to travel out to that spot beside the Serchio, but was held to those narrow rooms by my terrible weakness.

Four long and dreary weeks passed, until the middle of May, when I had gathered sufficient strength to walk out alone, and take short strolls in Oxford Street and its vicinity. Burton Blair's will had been proved, and Leighton, who visited us several times, told us of the recklessness with which the man Dawson was dealing with the estate. That the adventurer was in secret communication with Mabel was proved by the fact that certain cheques signed by her had passed through his hands into the bank, yet strangely enough, he declared entire ignorance of her whereabouts.

Dawson had returned to Grosvenor Square, when one day at noon the footman, Carter, was ushered in to me by Glave.

I saw by his face that the man was excited, and scarcely had he been shown into my room before he exclaimed, saluting respectfully—

"I've found out Miss Mabel's address, sir! Ever since she's been gone I've kept my eyes on the letters sent to post, just as Mr. Ford suggested that I should, but Mr. Dawson never wrote to her until this morning, by accident I think, he sent a letter to the post addressed to her, among a number of others which he gave to the page-boy. She's at the Mill House, Church Enstone, near Chipping Norton."

In quick delight I sprang to my feet. I thanked him, ordered Glave to give him a drink and left London by the half-past one train for Oxfordshire.

Just before five o'clock I discovered the Mill House, a grey, old-fashioned place standing back behind a high box hedge from the village street at Church Enstone, on the highroad from Aylesbury to Stratford. Before the house was a tiny lawn, bright with tulip borders and sweet-smelling narcissi.

A broad-spoken waiting-maid opened the door and ushered me into a small, low, old-fashioned room, where I surprised my love crouched in a big armchair, reading.

"Why? Mr. Greenwood!" she gasped, springing to her feet, pale and breathless, "you!"

"Yes," I said, when the girl had closed the door and we were alone, "I have found you at last, Mabel—at last!" and, advancing, I took both her small hands tenderly in mine. Then, carried away by the ecstasy of the moment, I looked straight into her eyes, saying, "You have tried to escape me, but to-day I have found you again. I have come, Mabel, to confess openly to you, to tell you something—to tell you, dearest, that—well, that I love you!"

"Love me!" she cried, dismayed, starting back, and putting me from her with both her small, white hands. "No! no!" she wailed. "You must not—you cannot love me. It is impossible!"

"Why?" I demanded quickly. "I have loved you ever since that first night when we met. Surely you must long ago have detected the secret of my heart."

"Yes," she faltered, "I have. But alas! it is too late—too late!"

"Too late?" I exclaimed. "Why?"

She was silent. Her countenance had suddenly blanched to the lips, and I saw that she was trembling from head to foot.

I repeated my question seriously, my eyes fixed upon her.

"Because," she answered slowly at last in a tremulous voice so low that I could scarce distinguish the fatal words she uttered, "because I am already married!"

"Married!" I gasped, standing rigid. "And your husband! His name!"

"Cannot you guess?" she asked. "The man you have already seen—Herbert Hales." Her eyes were cast down from me as though in shame, while her pointed chin sank upon her panting breast.

XXV

The Sacred Name

What could I say? What would you have said?

I was silent. I knew not what words to utter. This scoundrelly young groom, the ne'er-do-well son of the respectable old seafarer who spent the evening of his days at the crossways, was actually the husband of the millionaire's daughter! It seemed utterly incredible, yet, on recollecting that midnight scene in Mayvill Park, I at once recognised how powerless she was in the hands of that low, arrogant cad, who, in a moment of mad frenzy, had made such a desperate attempt upon her.

I recognised, too, that the love between them, if any, had ever existed, had disappeared long ago, and that the man's sole idea was to profit by the fact of his union with her, and blackmail her just as so many wealthy and upright women are being blackmailed in England at this very moment. It flashed through my mind that the reason she did not follow and punish the fellow for that dastardly attempt on her life was now made plain.

She was his wife!

The very thought convulsed me with jealousy, regret and hatred, for I loved her with all the passion, honest and true, of which a man is capable. Since Mrs. Percival had revealed to me the truth, I had lived only for her, to meet her again and openly declare my love.

"Is this the truth?" I asked her at last in a voice the hardness of which I could not control. I took her cold, inert hand in my own and glanced at her bowed head.

"Alas for me it is," was her faltering response. "He is my husband, therefore all love between us is debarred," she added. "You have always been my friend, Mr. Greenwood, but now that you have forced me to confess the truth our friendship is at an end."

"And your husband, is he here with you?"

"He has been here," was her answer, "but has gone."

"You left London in secret to join him, I suppose?" I remarked bitterly.

"At his demand. He wished to see me."

"And to obtain money from you by threats as he attempted on that night at Mayvill?"

The broken, white-faced girl nodded in the affirmative.

"I came to this place," she explained, "as a paying-guest. A girl I knew at school, Bessie Wood, lives here with her mother. They believe I made a runaway match, and have been extremely kind to me these last two years."

"Then you've been a wife for two whole years!" I exclaimed in blank surprise, utterly amazed at the manner in which I had been deceived.

"For nearly that time. We were married at Wymondham in Norfolk."

"Tell me the whole story, Mabel," I urged, after a long pause, endeavouring to preserve an outward calm, which certainly did not coincide with my innermost feelings.

Her breast heaved and fell beneath its lace and chiffons, her great wonderful eyes were filled with tears. For fully five minutes she was overcome by her emotion and quite unable to speak. At last, in a low, hoarse voice, she said—

"I don't know what you must think of me, Mr. Greenwood. I'm ashamed of myself, and of the manner in which I've deceived you. My only excuse is that it was imperative. I married because I was forced to by a chain of circumstances, as you will realise when you know the truth." Then she was silent again.

"But you'll tell me the truth, won't you?" I urged. "I, as your best friend, as indeed the man who has loved you, have surely a right to know!"

She only shook her head in bitter sorrow, and looking at me through her tears, answered briefly—

"I have told you the truth. I am married. I can only ask your pardon for deceiving you and explain that I was compelled to do so."

"You mean that you were compelled to marry him? Compelled by whom?"

"By him," she faltered. "One morning two years ago I left London alone and met him at Wymondham, where I had previously been staying for a fortnight while my father was fishing. Herbert met me at the station, and we were married in secret, two men, picked at haphazard from the street, acting as witnesses. After the ceremony we parted. I took off my ring and returned home, no one being the wiser. We had a dinner-party that evening. Lord Newborough, Lady Rainham and yourself were there, and we went to the Haymarket afterwards. Don't you recollect it? As we sat in the box you asked me why I was so dull and thoughtful, and I pleaded a headache. Ah! if you had but known!"

"I recollect the night perfectly," I said, pitying her. "And it was your wedding evening? But how did he compel you to marry him? The motive is, of course, quite plain. He wished either to profit by the fact that you could not afford to allow the truth to be known that you were the wife of a groom, or else his intention was to gain possession of your money at your father's death. Yours is certainly not the first marriage of the sort that has been contracted," I added, with a feeling of blank dismay.

At the very moment when my hopes had been raised to their highest level by Mrs. Percival's statement the blow had fallen, and in an instant I saw that love was impossible. Mabel, the woman I loved so fondly and so well, was the wife of a loutish brute who was torturing her to madness by his threats, and would, as already had been proved, hesitate at nothing in order to gain his despicable ends.

My feelings were indescribable. No words of mine can give any adequate idea of how torn was my heart by conflicting emotions. Until that moment she had been beneath my protection, yet now that she was the wife of another I had no right to control her actions, no right to admire, no right to love.

Ah! if ever man felt crushed, despairing and hopeless, if ever man realised how aimless and empty his lonely life had been, I did at that moment.

I tried to induce her to tell me how the fellow had compelled her to marry him, but the words stuck in my throat and choked me. Tears must, I suppose, have stood in my eyes, for with a sudden sympathy, an outburst of that womanly feeling so strong within her, she placed her hand tenderly upon my shoulder and said in a low, calm voice—

"We cannot recall the past, therefore why reflect? Act as I asked you to act in my letter. Forgive me and forget. Leave me to my own sorrows. I know now that you have loved me, but it is—"

She could not finish the sentence, for she burst into tears.

"I know what you mean," I said blankly. "Too late—yes, too late. Both our lives have been wrecked by my own folly—because I hid from you what I as an honest man, should have told you long ago."

"No, no, Gilbert," she cried, calling me for the first time by my Christian name, "don't say that. The fault is not yours, but mine—mine," and she covered her face with her hands and sobbed aloud.

"Where is this husband of yours—this man who tried to kill you?" I demanded fiercely a few moments later.

"Somewhere in the North, I think."

"He has been here. When?"

"He came a week ago and remained a couple of hours."

"But he shall not blackmail you in this manner! If I cannot remain your lover. I'll nevertheless still stand your champion, Mabel!" I cried in determination. "He shall reckon with me."

"Ah no!" she gasped, turning to me in quick apprehension. "You must do nothing. Otherwise he may—"

"What may he do?"

She was silent, gazing aimlessly out of the window across the broad meadow-lands, now misty and silent in the dusk.

"He may," she said, in a low, broken voice, "he may tell the world the truth!"

"What truth?"

"The truth he knows—the knowledge by which he compelled me to become his wife," and she held her hand to her breast, as though to stay the wild beating of her young heart.

I tried to induce her to reveal that secret to me, her most devoted friend, but she refused.

"No," she said in a low, broken voice, "do not ask me, Gilbert—for I know now that I may be permitted to call you by your Christian name—because I cannot tell you of all men. It is for me to remain silent—and to suffer."

Her face was very pale, and I saw by her look of determination that her mind was made up; even though she trusted me as she did, nevertheless no power would induce her to reveal the truth to me.

"But you know what reason your father had in appointing his friend Dawson to be controller of your fortune," I said. "I felt confident that a word from you would result in his withdrawal from the office he now holds. You cannot affect ignorance of this mysterious motive of your father's?"

"I have already told you. My poor father also acted under compulsion. Mr. Leighton also knows that."

"And you are aware of the reason?"

She nodded in the affirmative.

"Then you could checkmate the fellow's plans?"

"Yes, I might," she answered slowly, "if I only dared."

"What do you fear?"

"I fear what my father feared," was her answer.

"And what was that?"

"That he would carry out a certain threat he has many times made to my father, and later to myself. He threatened me on the day I left home—he dared me to breathe a single word."

Yes, that one-eyed man held power complete and absolute over her, just as he had boasted to Mrs. Percival. He also knew the truth concerning the Cardinal's secret.

We sat together in that small, low, old-fashioned room, until dusk darkened into night, when she rose wearily and lit the lamp. Then I was startled by discovering by its light how her sweet face had changed. Her cheeks had grown wan and pale, her eyes were red and swollen, and her whole countenance betrayed a deep, burning anxiety a terror of what the unknown future held for her.

Surely hers was a strange, almost inconceivable position—a pretty young woman with a balance of over two millions at her bankers, and yet hounded by those who sought her ruin, degradation and death.

The fact that she was married had struck me a staggering blow. To her I could now be no more than a mere friend like any other man, all thoughts of love being bebarred, all hope of happiness abandoned. I had never sought her for her fortune, that I can honestly avow. I had loved her for her own sweet, pure self, because I knew that her heart beat true and loyal; that in strength of character, in disposition, in grace and in beauty she was peerless.

For a long time I held her hand, feeling, I think, some satisfaction in thus repeating the action of other times, now that I had to bid farewell to all my hopes and aspirations. She sat silent, troubled sighs escaping her as I spoke, telling her of that strange, midnight adventure in the streets of Kensington, and of how near I had been to death.

"Then, knowing that you have gained the secret written upon the cards, they have made an attempt to seal your lips," she said at last, in a hard, mechanical voice, almost as though speaking to herself. "Ah! did I not warn you of that in my letter? Did I not tell you that the secret is so well and ingeniously guarded that you will never succeed in either learning it or profiting by it?"

"But I intend to persevere in the solution of the mystery of your father's fortune," I declared, still with her hand in mine, in sad and bitter farewell. "He left his secret to me, and I have determined to start out to Italy to-morrow to search the spot indicated, and to learn the truth."

"Then you can just save yourself that trouble, mister," exclaimed the voice of a common, uneducated man, startling me, and on turning suddenly, I saw that the door had opened noiselessly, and there upon the threshold, watching us with apparent satisfaction, was the man who stood between me and my well-beloved—that clean-shaven, skulking fellow who claimed her by the sacred name of wife!

XXVI

FACE TO FACE

I'd much like to know what your business is 'ere?" demanded the coarse-featured fellow, whose grey bowler hat and gaiters gave him a distinctly horsey appearance. And as he stood in the doorway, he folded his arms defiantly and looked me straight in the face.

"My business is my own affair," I answered, facing him in disgust.

"If it concerns my wife, I have a right to know," he persisted.

"Your wife!" I cried, advancing towards him, with difficulty repressing the strong impulse within me to knock the young ruffian down. "Don't call her your wife, fellow! Call her by her true name—your victim!"

"Do you mean that as an insult?" he exclaimed quickly, his face turning white with sudden anger, whereupon Mabel, seeing his threatening attitude, sprang between us and begged me to be calm.

"There are some men whom no words can insult," I replied forcibly. "And you are one of them."

"What do you mean?" he cried. "Do you wish to pick a quarrel?" and he came forward with clenched fists.

"I desire no quarrel," was my quick response. "I only order you to leave this lady in peace. She may be legally your wife, but I will stand as her protector."

"Oh!" he sneered, with curling lip. "And I'd like to know by what right you interfere between us?"

"By the common right every man has to shield an unprotected and persecuted woman," I replied, firmly. "I know you, and am well aware of your shameful past. Shall I recall one incident, that, now you attempt to defy me, you appear to have conveniently forgotten? Do you not recollect a certain night in the park at Mayvill not so very long ago, and do you not recollect that you there attempted to commit a foul and brutal murder—eh?"

He started quickly, then glared at me with the fire of a murderous hatred in his eyes.

"She's told you, damn her! She's given me away!" he exclaimed, with a contemptuous glance at his trembling wife.

"No, she has not," was my response. "I myself chanced to be witness of your dastardly attempt upon her. It was I who succeeded in rescuing her from the river. For that action of yours you must now answer to me."

"What do you mean?" he inquired, and from the lines in his countenance I saw that my outspoken manner caused him considerable uneasiness.

"I mean that it is not for you to attempt defiance, having regard to the fact that, had it not been for the fortunate circumstance of my presence in the park, you would to-day be a murderer."

He shrank at that final word. Like all his class, he was arrogant and overbearing to the weak, but as easily cowed by firmness as a dog who cringes at his master's voice.

"And now," I continued, "I may as well tell you that, on the night when you would have killed this poor woman who is your victim, I also overheard your demands. You are a blackmailer—the meanest and worst type of criminal humanity—and you seem to have forgotten that there is a severe and stringent law against such an offence as yours. You demanded money by threats, and on refusal made a desperate endeavour to take your wife's life. In the assize court the evidence I could give against you would put you into a term of penal servitude— you understand? Therefore I'll make this compact with you; if you will promise not to molest your wife further, I will remain silent."

"And who the deuce are you, pray, to talk to me in this manner—like a gaol chaplain on his weekly round!"

"You'd better keep a civil tongue, fellow, and just reflect upon my words," I said. "I'm no man for argument. I act."

"Act just as you like. I shall do as I think proper—you hear?"

"And you'll take the risk? Very well," I said. "You know the worst— prison."

"And you don't," he laughed. "Otherwise you wouldn't talk like a silly idiot. Mabel is my wife, and you've no say in the matter, so that's enough for you," he added insultingly. "Instead of trying to threaten me, it is I who have a right to demand why I find you here—with her."

"I'll tell you!" I cried angrily, my hands itching to give the impudent young blackguard a sound good hiding. "I'm here to protect her, because she is in fear of her life. And I shall remain here until you have gone."

"But I'm her husband, therefore I shall stay," sneered the fellow, perfectly unmoved.

"Then she leaves with me," I said decisively.

"I'll not allow that."

"You will act just as I think proper," I exclaimed. Then, turning to Mabel, who had remained white, silent and trembling, in fear lest we should come to blows, I said, "Put on your hat and coat at once. You must return to London with me."

"She shall not!" he cried, unflinchingly. "If my curses could blast yer you'd have 'em thick."

"Mabel," I said, taking no notice of the ruffian's words, but drawing back to allow her to pass out, "please get your coat. I have a fly waiting outside."

The fellow made a movement as though to prevent her leaving the room, but in an instant my hand was heavily upon his shoulder, and by my face he saw that I was strong and determined.

"You'll repent this!" he hissed threateningly, with an imprecation, between his teeth. "I know what you are searching for—but," he laughed, "you'll never obtain that secret which gave Blair his millions. You think you've a clue to it, but before long you'll discover your mistake."

"In what?"

"In not uniting with me, instead of insulting me."

"I have no necessity for the assistance of any man who would kill a helpless woman," I responded. "Recollect that in this affair you hold aloof from her, or, by Gad! without further ado, I'll seek the aid of the police, when your past history will prove rather unwelcome evidence of character."

"Do what you like," he laughed again defiantly. "By giving me over to the police you'll only be doing her the worst turn possible. If you doubt me, you'd better ask her. Be careful how you act before you make a fool of yourself and a victim of her." And with this harsh, hollow sneer he threw himself into the armchair and placed his feet on the fender in an attitude of carelessness and calmly lit a cheap, rank cigar.

"There will be only one sufferer, never fear," I said meaningly. "And that will be yourself."

"All right," he said, "we shall see."

Then turning I left the room, and meeting Mabel, who stood ready dressed in the hall, whispering a hurried adieu to Bessie Wood, her old schoolfellow, I hurried her out, put her into the station fly, and drove with her back to Chipping Norton.

Even then, however, I could not understand the exact position of that young ruffian, Herbert Hales, or the true meaning of his final ominous words of open defiance.

For the present I had rescued my love from the arrogant, cold-blooded brute and blackmailer, but for how brief a space I dreaded to anticipate. My own position, utterly in the dark as I remained, was one of uncertainty and insecurity. I loved Mabel, but now had no right to do so. She was already the wife, alas! the victim, of a man of low type and of criminal instinct.

Our journey up to Paddington was uneventful, and in almost complete silence. Both our hearts, beating sadly, were too full for mere words. The insurmountable barrier had fallen between us; we were both grief-stricken and heart-broken. The hopeful past had ended, the future was one of dull and dark despair.

On arrival in London she expressed a desire to see Mrs. Percival, and as she declined to return beneath the same roof as Dawson, I took her to the *York Hotel* in Albemarle Street, then, re-entering the cab, I drove to Grosvenor Square, where I informed the chaperon of my lost love's whereabouts.

Not an instant did Mrs. Percival delay in seeking her, and at midnight, accompanied by Reggie, I called again at the hotel, giving her certain injunctions to refuse to see her husband, even if he discovered her, and taking a lingering farewell of her, as we had arranged to leave Charing Cross for Italy by the mail at nine o'clock on the following morning.

Both Reggie and I had arrived at the conclusion that, now I was sufficiently recovered to travel, we should not lose an instant in going out to Tuscany, and investigating the truth regarding that cipher record.

So she bade us both farewell, and urging us not to worry further upon her account, although we did not fail to detect her wild anxiety as to the result of my defiance of her ruffianly husband, she wished us all good fortune and Godspeed in the exciting venture we were about to undertake, with success and a safe return.

XXVII

The Directions of His Eminence

The green, winding valley of the Serchio looks its brightest and best in the month of May the time of flowers in old-world Italy. Far removed from the great routes over which the English, Americans and Germans swarm in winter, unvisited, unknown and unexplored by any save the simple *contadini* of the hills, the rippling river winds with tortuous bends around sharp angles and beneath overhanging trees, great cliffs and huge grey boulders worn smooth by the action of the water of ages. In those lonely reaches of the river as it dashes on with many cascades from the giant Apennines to the sea, the brilliant kingfisher and the stately heron are in possession, and live their lives undisturbed by human intrusion. As we walked on, having left the carriage that had brought us up from Lucca at the quaint mediaeval bridge called the Ponte del Diavolo, the rural, quiet and picturesque beauty of the scene became impressed upon us. The silence was unbroken, save for the hum of the myriad insects in the sun, and the low music of the water which at that point is shallow, running over its rocky bed.

On arrival at the *Universo* in Lucca, my first impulse was to go up to the monastery and see Fra Antonio. Yet so intimate did he appear to be with Blair's partner, the ex-boatswain Dawson, that we resolved to first explore the spot and take some observations. Therefore at eight that morning we had entered one of those dusty old travelling Tuscan carriages, the horses of which bore many jingling bells, and now, as noon was approaching, we found ourselves on the left bank of the river, counting the four hundred and fifty-six foot-paces as directed by the secret record upon the cards.

To avoid being watched by our driver, to whom we had given instructions to go back to a little wayside trattoria, or eating-house, which we had passed, but who we knew would endeavour to secretly watch our movements, we were at first compelled, on account of the absence of a path, to make a detour through a small wood, rejoining the river bank at some distance further up.

Therefore, as we reached the water, standing amid the high undergrowth that grew upon the banks, we could only look back at the bridge and guess that we were about one hundred foot-paces from it.

Then, tramping steadily forward in single file we pushed our way with difficulty through the tall grass, briars, giant ferns and tangled creepers, slowly onward towards the spot indicated. In places the trees met overhead, and the sun shining through the foliage struck the rippling water with pretty effect.

According to the record the spot must be in the open, for the sun shone upon it for one hour at noon on the fifth of April and for two hours on the fifth of May. It was now the nineteenth of May, therefore the duration of the sunshine would, we roughly calculated, be about a quarter of an hour longer.

In some places the river was open to the sun, while in others, so high were the banks on either side, the light could never penetrate there. From the crevices of the overhanging rocks, mountain pines and other trees had taken root and grown to huge size, bending over until their branches almost swept the stream, while our progress was made slower and more difficult by the unevenness of the bank and the wild tangle of the undergrowth.

One fact was proved—no one had approached the spot for a considerable time, for we found not a twig severed or a leaf disturbed by previous intruders.

At last, after we had climbed high along a rocky cliff that descended sheer into the water, and had calculated four hundred and twenty steps from the old pointed bridge, we suddenly rounded a bend in the river and came upon a space where the stream, still a hundred feet or so below, broadened out, so that it lay open to the sky for forty yards or so.

"It must be here!" I cried in eager anticipation, halting and quickly surveying the spot. "The directions are to descend twenty-four foot-holes. I suppose that means steps cut in the rock. We must find them." And both of us began to search eagerly, but in that tangled growth we could discover no trace of them.

"The record says that we go down behind where a man can hold himself against four hundred," exclaimed Reggie, reading from a copy of the transcript which he took from his pocket. "That appears as if the entry is in some narrow crevice between two rocks. Do you see any such likely spot?"

I looked eagerly around but was compelled to admit that I discerned nothing that coincided with the description.

So sheer was the grey limestone cliff, going down to the water, that I approached its edge with caution and then, throwing myself upon my stomach, I crept forward and peered over its insecure edge. In doing so a huge piece of rock became loosened and fell with a roar and splash into the stream.

I took careful observations, but could distinguish absolutely nothing to correspond with what the old outlaw, Poldo Pensi, had recorded.

For a full half-hour we searched in vain, until it became plain that, as we had not measured accurately the foot-paces from the Devil's Bridge, we were not at the exact spot. We therefore retraced our steps slowly and laboriously through the tangled briars and undergrowth, our clothes suffering considerably, and then restarted from the actual base of the bridge. So completely had we been out of reckoning that at the three hundred and eighty-seventh pace we passed the spot where we had made such minute search, and continuing our way forward we halted at the four hundred and fifty-sixth foot-pace in the top of a high encampment very similar to the other, only wilder and even more inaccessible.

"There seems nothing here," remarked Reggie, whose face was torn by brambles and was bleeding.

I gazed around and was reluctantly compelled to endorse his statement. The trees were large and shady where we stood, some of them overhanging the deep chasm through which the river wound. Cautiously, we both crept forward, flat upon our stomachs, to the edge of the cliff, taking that precaution as we knew not whether the edge might be rotten, and presently we peered over.

"Why, look!" cried my friend, pointing to a spot about half-way down the deep swirling stream as it came round the sudden bend, "there's steps and a path leading down just a little higher up. And see! what's that?"

XXVIII

Describes a Startling Discovery

I looked and saw that upon a kind of natural platform on the rock was built a small stone hut, upon the grey-tiled roof of which we were gazing down.

"Yes, there are the 'twenty-four foot-holes' mentioned in the record, no doubt," I said. "I wonder if anybody lives down there."

"Well, let's descend and investigate," suggested Reggie anxiously, and a few moments later we had struck a narrow track leading from the chestnut wood direct to the roughly-cut steps that went down to a narrow opening between two rocks. Upon the right hand one we found deeply graven an old-fashioned capital E, about a foot long, and passing by it we saw that a rough and perilous track led zigzag down to the small hut, the closed door and small barred window of which caused us the wildest curiosity as to what was within.

Next moment, however, the truth was plain. The front of the little place was pointed, and upon the apex was a small stone cross.

It was a hermit's cell, like so many similar ancient places of retreat and contemplation in old-world Italy, and an instant later, as we passed the rocks and came cautiously down the path, the door opened, and there issued forth the hermit himself, who, to my surprise, I recognised as no other person than the burly, dark-bearded monk, Antonio!

"Gentlemen," he exclaimed, speaking in Italian, as he greeted us, "this is certainly an unexpected meeting," and he indicated the stone bench that ran along the outside of the low little hut, which I saw was so cunningly concealed by the overhanging trees as to be invisible either from the river or from the opposite bank. As we seated ourselves at his direction, he hitched up his faded brown habit beneath his waist-cord and himself sat down beside us.

I expressed surprise at finding him there, but he only smiled, saying—

"You are disappointed at discovering nothing else—eh?"

"We expected to reveal the secret of the Cardinal Sannini," was my frank response, well knowing that he was in possession of the truth, and suspecting that, with the one-eyed Englishman, he had been partner with Blair.

The monk's strongly-marked, sunburnt features assumed a puzzled expression, for he saw that we had gained some knowledge, yet he hesitated to make inquiry lest he should betray himself. Capuchins, like Jesuits, are wonderful diplomatists. Doubtless, the monk's personal fascination was somewhat due to his splendid presence. A man of fine physique, he had a handsome, open face, with clean-cut, powerful features, softened by eyes in which seemed the light of perpetual youth, with a candid, unassuming expression, brightened by a twinkling humour about the lips.

"You have recovered the record, then," he remarked at last, looking straight into my face.

"Yes, and having read it," I answered, "I am here to investigate and claim the secret bequeathed to me."

He drew a long breath, glanced for an instant at both of us, and his shaggy black brows contracted. It was hot where we sat, for the brilliant Italian sun beat straight down upon us, therefore, without replying to me, he rose and invited us into his cool little cell, a square bare room with boarded floor, the furniture consisting of a low, old-fashioned wooden bedstead, with a piece of old brown blanket for coverlet, a Renaissance *prie-dieu* in old carved oak, black with age, a chair, a hanging lamp, and upon the wall a great crucifix.

"Well, and the Signor Dawson?" he asked at last, when Reggie had seated himself on the edge of the bed, and I had taken the chair. "What does he say?"

"I have no necessity to ask his opinion," I responded quickly. "By law the Cardinal's secret is mine, and no one can dispute it."

"Except its present holder," was his quiet remark.

"Its present holder has no right to it. Burton Blair has made gift of it to me, and it is therefore mine," I declared.

"I do not dispute that," answered the dark-faced monk. "But as guardian of the Cardinal's secret, I have a right to know the manner in which the record upon the cards came into your hands, and how you gained the key to the cipher."

I related to him exactly what he wished to ascertain, whereupon he answered—

"You have certainly succeeded where I anticipated that you would fail, and your presence here to-day surprises me. Apparently you have overcome every obstacle, and are now here to claim from me what is undoubtedly yours by right." He seemed fair-minded, yet I confess

I was loth to trust men of his stamp very far, and was therefore still suspicious.

"Before we go further, however," he said, standing with his hands in the wide sleeves of his habit, "I would ask whether it is your intention to continue the methods of the Signor Blair, who allotted one-eighth part of the money derived from the secret to our Order of Capuchins?"

"Certainly," I answered, rather surprised. "My desire is to regard in every particular my dead friend's obligations."

"Then that is a promise," he said with some eagerness. "You make that solemnly—you take an oath? Raise your hand!" And he pointed to the great crucifix upon the white-washed wall.

I raised my hand and exclaimed—

"I swear to act as Burton Blair has acted."

"Very well," answered the monk, apparently satisfied that I was a man of honour. "Then I suppose the secret, strange as it will strike you, must now be revealed to you. Think, Signore, at this moment you are a comparatively poor man, yet in half an hour you will be rich beyond your wildest dreams—worth millions, just as Burton Blair became."

I listened to him, scarcely believing my ears. Yet what was the possession of riches to me, now that I had lost my love?

From a little cupboard he took a small, rusty old hurricane lamp, and carefully lit it, while we both watched with breathless interest. Then he closed the door and securely locked and barred it, afterwards placing the shutters to the iron-barred window, so that we were quickly in darkness. Was some supernatural illusion about to be shown us? We stood open-mouthed in expectation.

A moment later he dragged his low ponderous bedstead away from the corner, where we saw that in the floor was a cunningly-concealed trap-door, which, on being lifted, disclosed a deep, dark, well-like hole beneath.

"Be careful," he cautioned us, "the steps are rather difficult in places," and holding the lantern he soon disappeared, leaving us to follow him down a roughly-hewn spiral flight of foot-holes in the stone, deeper and deeper into the solid rock, damp and slimy in places where the water percolated through and fell in loudly-sounding drops.

"Bend low!" ordered our guide, and we saw the faint glimmer of this lamp lighting our path along a narrow, tortuous burrow which ran away at right angles and sloped down still further into the heart of the cliff. In places we went through a veritable quagmire of mud and slime, while the close atmosphere smelt foul and earthy.

Suddenly we emerged into a great opening, the dimensions of which we could not ascertain with that one single glimmering light.

"These caverns run for miles," explained the monk. "The galleries run in all directions right under the city of Lucca and over towards the Arno. They have never been explored. Listen!"

In the weird darkness we heard the distant roaring of tumbling waters far away.

"That is the subterranean river, the stream that divides the secret from all men save yourself," he said. Then he went forward again, keeping along one side of the gigantic cavern through which we were passing, and we followed, approaching nearer those thundering waters, until at last he told us to halt, and appeared to be examining the rough walls upon which shone great glittering stalactites.

Presently he found a large white mark similar to the letter E on the rock upon the cliff-side, and placed his lantern on the floor.

"Don't move another step forward," he said. Then he produced from a hole, where it appeared to be well hidden, a long, roughly-made footbridge, consisting of a single plank, with a light handrail on each side. This he pushed before him while I held the lantern, until he came to the edge of a deep chasm and then bridged it across so that we could pass over.

When in the centre, he held aloft the lantern, and as we peered down a hundred feet we shuddered to see, deep down in the chasm, the rushing flood of black water roaring away into the bowels of the earth, a terrible trap to those who ventured to explore that weird, dank place.

Having passed safely over we again skirted a wall of rock to the right, traversed a long, narrow tunnel and at last emerged into another open space, of the dimensions of which we could gather no idea.

Here the monk set down his lantern in a niche wherein stood several candles stuck upon rude boards and secured between three nails. When they were lit and our eyes grew accustomed to the light, we saw that the chamber was not a large one, but that it was long, narrow and somewhat drier than the rest.

"See!" exclaimed the Capuchin, with a wave of his hand. "It is all there, Signor Greenwood, and all yours."

Then I realised to my utter amazement that around the walls of the place, piled high, one on the other, were sacks of untanned hide filled to bursting. One pile close to my hand I touched, and found that what was within them was hard, angular and unyielding. There were many small, old-fashioned chests which, from their strong appearance, banded with rusted iron and studded with nails, must, I knew, contain the mysterious riches that raised Burton Blair from homeless wayfarer to millionaire.

"Why, surely this is an actual hoard of treasure!" I cried.

"Yes," answered Fra Antonio in his deep, bass voice. "The hidden treasure of the Vatican. See," he added, "it is all here except that portion taken out by the Signor Blair," and opening one of the massive chests, he held his lantern above and displayed such a miscellaneous collection of golden chalices, monstrances, patens, jewel-embroidered vestments and magnificent gems, such as had never before dazzled my eyes.

Both Reggie and I stood utterly dumbfounded. At first I seemed to be living in some fairy world of legend and romance, but when a moment later the rugged, bearded face of the Capuchin recalled to me all the past, I stood open-mouthed in wonder.

The secret of Burton Blair was disclosed—and the secret was now mine!

"Ah!" exclaimed the monk, laughing, "no doubt this revelation is, to you, an amazing one. Did I not, however, promise you that in half an hour you would become many times over a millionaire?"

"Yes; but tell me the history of all this great wealth," I urged, for he had cut open one or two of the leathern bags, and I saw that each of them was filled with gold and gems mostly set in crucifixes and ornaments of an ecclesiastical character.

XXIX

In which a Strange Tale is Told

I suppose it is only just that you should now know the truth, although a most strenuous effort has been made to keep it from you," the monk remarked, as though to himself. "Well, it is this. You, as a Protestant, probably know that the treasures in the Vatican in Rome are the greatest in the world, and also that each Pope, on his jubilee or other notable anniversary, receives a vast number of presents, while the church of St. Peter's itself is constantly in receipt of quantities of ornaments and jewels as votive offerings. These are preserved in the treasury of the Vatican, and constitute a collection of wealth unequalled by all the millions of modern millionaires. Well, in the early part of 1870, Pope Pius IX received, through the marvellous diplomatic channels our Holy Church possesses, secret information that it was the intention of the Italian troops to bombard and enter Rome, and sack the Palace of the Vatican. His Holiness confided his fears to his favourite, the great, Cardinal Sannini, the treasurer-general, who, having lived in this district when a peasant lad, was aware of the existence of this safe hiding-place. He, therefore, succeeded, during the months of June, July and August 1870, in secretly removing a vast quantity of the Vatican treasure from Rome and storing it in this place in order to save it from the enemy's hands. True to the fears of His Holiness, on September 20 the Italian troops, after a five days' bombardment, entered Rome, but, fortunately, no serious attack was made upon the Vatican, while the treasure removed has remained here ever since. Cardinal Sannini was, it appears, a traitor to the Church, for although he induced Pio Nono to allow the treasure to be removed in secret, he never told him the exact spot where it was concealed, and curiously enough the two members of the Swiss Guard who had assisted the Cardinal, and alone knew the secret, both disappeared—in all probability, I believe, precipitated into that subterranean river we have just crossed. Originally, the small entrance to these galleries was only hidden by brambles, but, directly after the treasure had been safely secreted, His Eminence the Cardinal suddenly discovered that the spot on the cliff-side was well adapted for a hermitage, and he built the present hut over the small opening in the rock in order to conceal it, having first closed the hole with his own hands so that the stone-masons should not discover the entrance. For many months, during the struggle between, the Italian Government and the Holy See, he doffed the purple and lived in the cell, a hermit, but in reality guarding the enormous treasure he had so cleverly secured. But, as you know, he was captured by the terrible Poldo Pensi, dreaded down in Calabria, and was compelled, in order to save his life and reputation, to betray the existence of his hoard. Upon this, Pensi came here in secret, saw the treasure, but being extremely superstitious, as are all his class, he dare not touch one single object. A man who had once served in his band and who had entered our monastery, a certain Fra Orazio, he sought out, and to him gave the hermitage, without, however, telling him of the secret tunnel and caves beneath. Both Sannini and the Pope died, but Fra Orazio, in ignorance of the fact that he resided over a veritable mine of wealth, continued here sixteen years, until he died, and I succeeded him in the occupancy of the cell, spending nearly six months each year here in meditation and prayer.

"In the meantime, however, the secret of His Eminence inscribed in the secret cipher used by the Vatican in the seventeenth century, seems to have passed through Poldo Pensi into the hands of Burton Blair, his shipmate and intimate friend. The first I knew of it was about five years ago, when one day my peace was disturbed by a visit from two Englishmen, Blair and Dawson. They told me a story of the secret being given to them, but at first I would not believe that there was any truth in the hidden hoard. We, however, investigated, and after a very long, difficult and perilous search we succeeded in revealing the truth."

"Then Dawson shared in the secret, as well as in the profits?" I remarked, astounded at the amazing truth.

"Yes, the three of us alone knew the secret, and it was then mutually arranged that it having been given by the repentant brigand to Blair, he was entitled to the greater share, while Dawson, to whom Pensi had apparently spoken before his death concerning the treasure, and who had been in possession of certain facts, should be allotted one quarter of the annual out-take, and to myself, appointed guardian of the treasure-house, one eighth to be paid, not to myself direct, as that would arouse suspicion, but by Blair's bankers in London to the Vicar-General of the Order of the Capuchins at Rome. Through five years this arrangement has been carried out. Once every six months we entered this chamber in company and selected a certain amount of gems and other articles of value which were sent by certain channels—the gems to Amsterdam for sale and the other articles to the great auction-rooms of Paris, Brussels and London, and others into the hands of renowned dealers in antiques. As you may see for yourself, this collection of gems is almost inexhaustible. Three rubies alone fetched sixty-five thousand pounds in Paris last year, while some of the emeralds have realised enormous sums, yet so ingeniously did the Signori Dawson and Blair arrange the channels by which they were placed upon the market that none ever guessed the truth."

"But all this is, strictly speaking, the property of the Church of Rome," remarked Reggie.

"No," answered the big monk in his broken English; "according to Cardinal Sannini, His Holiness, after the peace with Italy, made a free gift to him of the whole of it as a mark of regard, and knowing too that with Rome in the occupation of the Italian troops it would be difficult to get the great collection of jewels back again into the treasury without exciting suspicion."

"Then all this is mine!" I exclaimed, even then unable to fully realise the truth.

"All," answered the monk, "except the share to me, or rather to my Order, for distribution to the poor, as payment for its guardianship, and that to the Signor Dawson—with, I suppose," and he turned towards Reggie, "some acknowledgment to your friend. I warned you against him once," he added, "but it was owing to what Dawson told me—lies."

"I have already pledged myself to continue to act towards your Order as Burton Blair has done," I replied. "As to Dawson that is another matter, but certainly my friend Seton here will not be forgotten, nor you personally, as the faithful holder of the secret."

"Any reward of mine goes to my Order," was the manly fellow's quiet reply. "We are forbidden to possess money, our small personal wants being supplied by the father superior, and of this world's riches we desire none save that necessary to relieve the poor and afflicted."

"You shall have some for that purpose, never fear," I laughed.

Then, as the air exhausted by the lights seemed to grow more foul, we decided to return to the cell so cunningly constructed at the mouth of the narrow outer gallery.

We had reached the brink of that terrible abyss where the black flood roared deep below, and I had passed over the narrow hand-bridge and gained the opposite side safely, when, without warning, a pair of strong hands seized me in the darkness, and almost ere I could utter a cry I was forced backwards to the edge of the awful chasm.

The hands held me in an iron grip by the throat and arm, and so suddenly had I been seized that for the first instant I believed it to be a joke on Reggie's part—for he was fond of horseplay when in jubilant spirits.

"My God!" I however heard him cry a second later, as I suppose the flickering lamplight fell upon my assailant's countenance, "why, it's Dawson!"

Knowledge of the terrible truth that I had been seized by my worst enemy, who had followed us in, well knowing the place, aroused within me a superhuman strength, and I grappled with the fellow in a fierce death struggle. Ere my two companions could reach and rescue me we were swaying to and fro in the darkness on the very edge of the abyss into which it was his intention to hurl me to the same death that the two Swiss Guards had probably been consigned by the wily cardinal.

I realised his murderous intention none too quickly, for with a fierce oath he panted—

"You sha'n't escape me now! That blow in the fog didn't have the desired effect, but once down there you'll never intrude again upon my affairs. Down you go!"

I felt my strength fail me as he forced me back still further, locked in his deadly embrace. In the darkness one of my companions gripped me and saved me, but at that instant I had recourse to an old Charterhouse trick, and twisting suddenly, so that my opponent stood in my place, I tripped him backwards, at the same moment slipping from his grasp.

It was the work of a second. In the uncertain glimmer from the lamp I saw him stumble, clutch wildly at the air, and with an awful cry of rage and despair he fell backwards, down into the Stygian blackness where the rushing waters swept him down to subterranean regions, unknown and unexplored.

My escape from death was assuredly the narrowest man had ever had, and I stood panting, breathless, bewildered, until Reggie took me by the arm and led me forward in silence more impressive than any words.

XXX

The Motive and the Moral

On the following night we took leave of the strong, big-handed monk on the railway platform in Lucca, and entered the train on the first stage of our journey back to England. He was to return at once to his hermit cell above the swirling Serchio, and remain, as before, the silent guardian of that great secret which, had it been revealed, would have astounded the world.

Anxiety consumed us, knowing not how Mabel had fared. Yet with the knowledge that the baneful influence of the adventurer Dawson had been now removed, we returned home somewhat easier in mind. I was wealthy, it was true, rich beyond my wildest dreams, yet the hope of the possession of Mabel as my wife, that had been the mainspring of my life, had been snapped, and in those pensive hours as the sleeping-car express tore northward across the plains of Lombardy and through Switzerland and France, my despairing thoughts were all of her and of her future.

A cab took us direct from Charing Cross to Great Russell Street, where I found a note from her dated from Grosvenor Square, asking me to call there on the instant of our return. This I did after a hasty wash, and Carter showed me unceremoniously and at once up to that big white-and-gold drawing-room so familiar to me.

In a few moments she entered, looking sweet and charming in her mourning, a smile upon her lips, her hand extended to me in glad welcome. Her face, I thought, betrayed a keen anxiety, and the pallor of her cheeks showed how sorely her heart was torn by grief and terror.

"Yes, Mabel, I am back again," I said, holding her hand and gazing into her eyes. "I have discovered your father's secret!"

"What?" she cried in eager surprise, "you have? Tell me what it is—do tell me," she urged breathlessly.

I first obtained from her a promise of secrecy, and then, standing with her, I described our visit to the lonely hermit's cell, our reception by the monk Antonio, and our subsequent discoveries.

She listened in blank amazement at my story of the hidden treasure of the Vatican, until I described the attack made upon me by Dawson, and its tragic sequel, whereupon she cried—

"Then if that man is dead—actually dead—I am free!"

"How? Explain!" I demanded.

"Well, now that circumstances have combined to thus liberate me, I will confess to you," she responded after a brief pause. Her face had suddenly flushed and glancing across at the door, she first reassured herself that it was closed. Then in a deep, intense voice she said, looking straight into my face with those wonderful eyes of hers, "I have been the victim of a foul, base plot which I will explain, so that, knowing the whole truth, you may be able to judge how I have suffered, and whether I have not acted from a sense of right and duty. For devilish cunning and ingenuity the conspiracy against me surely has no equal, as you will see. I have only now succeeded in discovering the real truth and the deep hidden motive behind it all. My first meeting with Herbert Hales was apparently accidental, in Widemarsh Street, Hereford. I was only a girl just finishing my schooldays, and as full of romantic ideas concerning men as all girls are. I saw him often, and although I knew that he picked up a precarious living on race-courses, I allowed him to court me. At first I confess that I fell deeply in love with him, a fact which he did not fail to detect, and during that summer at Mayvill I met him secretly on many evenings in the park. After we had thus been acquainted about three months, he one night suggested that we should marry, but by that time, having detected that his love for me was only feigned, I refused. Evening after evening we met, but I steadfastly declined to marry him, until one night he showed himself in his true colours, for to my abject amazement he told me that he was well acquainted with my father's life-story, and further he alleged that there was one dark incident connected with it—namely that my father, in order to possess himself of the secret by which he had gained his wealth, had murdered the Italian seaman, Pensi, on board the *Annie Curtis* off the Spanish coast. I refused to hear such a terrible allegation, but to my surprise he caused me to meet my father's friend, the man Dawson, by appointment, and the last-named declared that he was the actual witness of my father's crime. When we were alone that same night as we walked by a bypath across the park he put his intentions to me plainly—namely, that I should be compelled to accept him as my husband, and marry him is secret against my father's knowledge. Otherwise he would give information to the police regarding the allegation against my father."

"The blackguard!" I cried.

Continuing, she said, "He pointed out how Dawson, my father's closest friend, was the actual witness, and so completely did I find myself and my father's reputation in his unscrupulous hands, that I was compelled, after a week of vain resistance, to accept his condition of secrecy and consent to the odious marriage. From that moment, although I returned home the instant we were made man and wife, I was completely in his power, and had to pay blackmail to him at every demand. After he had secured me as his victim, his true passionate instincts—those of a man who lived by his wits and to whom a woman's heart was of no account—were almost instantly revealed, and from that moment until the present, although believed to be a single girl, and chaperoned to all sorts of functions in the brightest set in London, yet I lived in mortal terror of the man who was by law my husband."

She paused to gain breath, and I saw that her lips were white, and that she was trembling.

"Fortunately," she went on at last, "you were able to rescue me, otherwise the plot would have been successful in every particular. Until yesterday, I was entirely unaware of the real motive of forcing me into that marriage, but now it is revealed I can see the deep cunning of the master mind that planned it. Herbert Hales, it seems, first sought me out because of a chance remark of old Mr. Hales regarding my father's great and mysterious fortune. An adventurer, he saw that he might contract marriage with myself, as heiress to my father's possessions. When we had been acquainted about a month, Dawson chanced to be over from Italy, staying with us at Mayvill for a few days, and one evening while out shooting wood pigeons he discovered us walking together at the edge of the wood skirting the park. The instant he saw us he formed a devilish design, and next day, set about making inquiries regarding Hales, and, ascertaining the character of the man, met him and made a curious compact with him to the effect that if he, Dawson, so arranged matters that a secret marriage was contracted between myself and Hales, the latter was, in the case of my father's death, to receive the sum of two thousand a year in lieu of any claim against the estate on his wife's behalf. He pointed out to Hales that by a secret marriage with me he would obtain a source of continual revenue, as I dare not refuse his demands for money, because if I, on my part, exposed the secret of our union, he could at once take up his correct position as the husband of the millionaire's daughter. This having been arranged, he told Hales many true facts concerning my father's life at sea in order to mislead me, but added an allegation which, being corroborated by himself, I unfortunately believed to be true, that my father had committed murder in order to obtain that little pack of cards with the cipher upon them. Dawson, who had quickly judged the character of Hales, secretly aided him to get me completely in his power, although, of course, I was entirely unaware of it. His motive in securing my marriage in such compulsory circumstances was a far-seeing one, for he recognised that had I married the man I loved, my husband would, on my father's death, see that my rights as heiress were properly established, while if, on the other hand, I were Hales' wife, afraid to acknowledge my matrimonial *mesalliance*, and Hales was by the compact entirely in his power, he would in the end obtain complete possession of my father's money. He knew, of course, that his position as one of the holders of the secret of the Vatican treasure, as it now turns out to be, made it imperative for my father to leave the management of my affairs in his hands, and therefore he took every precaution to secure complete possession upon my poor father's death. The ingenious manner in which he secretly placed Herbert Hales in possession of certain facts which, I believed, were only known to my father and myself, the subtle manner in which he corroborated his own untruth, alleging that my father was guilty of a crime, and the secrecy with which he aided Hales to marry me under sheer compulsion were, I can now see, marvels of clever conspiracy. I feared, nay, I felt convinced all along, that the terrible secret of my father as known to Hales was the awful truth, and it is only yesterday that, with the aid of old Mr. Hales, I succeeded in discovering in a back street in Grimsby a man named Palmer, who was seaman on board the *Annie Curtis* and present at the Italian's death. He tells me that the allegation against my father is absolutely false, and that on the contrary he was the man's best and kindest friend, and in acknowledgment of this, the Italian gave him the little chamois leather bag containing the cards. My fears as to the secret having been obtained by foul play are therefore entirely set at rest; and the stain removed from my poor father's memory."

"But the mode of your father's death?" I said, amazed at this remarkable revelation of craft and deception.

"Ah!" she sighed, "my opinion has altered. He died from natural causes just at a moment when a secret attempt was to be made to assassinate him. By that same train up to Manchester, Herbert Hales—who was, of course, unknown to my father—and the man Dawson travelled in company, and I have no doubt that it was their intention if opportunity was afforded, to strike a blow with the same fatal knife with which the attempt was later made upon you. Death, however, cheated them of their victim."

"But this villainous scoundrel who is your husband? What of him?"

"The judgment of Heaven has already fallen upon him," was her low, almost mechanical answer. "What!" I gasped eagerly. "Is he dead?"

"He quarrelled here with Dawson on the night you left London, and again the one-eyed man exhibited that remarkable craft he possessed, for, in order to rid himself of Hales and the ugly facts of which he was in possession, he appears to have given confidential information to the police of a certain robbery committed about a year ago after Kempton Park races, in which the man from whom a large sum of money was stolen was so severely injured that he died. Two detectives went to Hales' lodgings in Lower Seymour Street about two o'clock in the morning. They demanded admittance to his room, but he, realising that Dawson had carried out his threat and that the truth was out, barricaded himself in. When they at last forced the door, they found him stretched dead upon the floor with a revolver lying beside him."

"Then you are free, Mabel—free to marry me!" I cried, almost beside myself with joy.

She hung her head, and answered in a tone so low that I could hardly catch the words—

"No, I am unworthy, Gilbert. I deceived you."

"The past is past, and all forgotten," I exclaimed, snatching up her hand, and bending until my hot, passionate lips touched hers. "You are mine, Mabel—mine alone!" I cried. "That is, of course, if you dare to trust your future in my hands."

"Dare!" she echoed, smiling through the tears which filled her eyes. "Have I not trusted you these past five years? Have you not indeed been always my best friend, from that night when we first met until this moment?"

"But have you sufficient regard for me, dearest?" I asked, deeply touched by her words. "I mean, do you love me?"

"I do, Gilbert," she faltered, with eyes downcast in modesty. "I have loved no man except yourself."

Then I clasped her to me, and in those moments of my new-born ecstasy I repeated to my love the oft-told tale—the tale that every man the world over tells the woman before whom he bows in adoration.

WILLIAM LE QUEUX

And what more need I say? A delicious sense of possession thrilled my heart. She was mine! mine for ever! I was convinced that in those terrible sufferings through which she had passed, she had been always loyal and true to me. She had, poor girl, like her father, been the innocent victim of the ingenious adventurer, Dawson, and the unscrupulous young blackguard who was his tool, and who had inveigled her into marriage in order to subsequently possess themselves of the whole of Blair's gigantic fortune.

The wheel of fortune, however, ran back upon them, and instead of success their own avarice and ingenuity resulted in their defeat, and at the same time placed me in the position they had intended to occupy.

XXXI

Conclusion

Mabel and I are now man and wife, and surely no couple in London are as perfectly happy as we are.

To us, after the storms and stress of life, has come a calm and blissful peace. The faithful Ford is back as my secretary, while we frequently chaff Reggie, who has sold his lace business, about his profound admiration of Dolly Dawson, who, even though the daughter of an adventurer, is, I am compelled to admit, a modest and most charming girl, who would, I feel sure, make my old chum an excellent life-partner. Indeed, the other day he inquired in strict confidence of Mrs. Percival, who has apartments with us at Mayvill, whether she thought Mabel would take it ill were he to propose. Therefore his ideas are evidently now running in the direction of matrimony. Old Hales still lives at the Crossway at Owston, and recently came with his wife to London to visit us.

As regards the Cardinal's secret, no word of it has ever leaked out to the public, it being far too carefully guarded by us. Over the entrance to that great storehouse of wealth the grave, black-bearded monk in the frayed habit, Fra Antonio, the friend of the poor of Lucca, still lives, dividing his lonely life between solitary meditation and attending to the wants of the destitute in that crowded city away down the green valley.

The Church of Rome has a long memory. For years, it seems, active steps have been in progress to search and recover the great treasure given by Pius IX to his favourite Sannini. The presence in London of the well-known cleric, Monsignore Galli, of Rimini, and his clandestine interview with Dolly, was, according to her own avowal, in order to ascertain some facts regarding her father's recent movements, it being known that he had a few months before sold to a dealer in Paris the historic jewelled crucifix worn by Clement VIII which was placed in the Vatican treasury after his death in 1605.

Many men in the City are aware of the great fortune that has come to me, and you yourself are perhaps acquainted with the white exterior of one house in Grosvenor Square, yet none assuredly know the strange facts which I have here for the first time put on record.

A month ago I was seated in that silent little cell which so cunningly conceals the vast wealth of which I am now possessor and which has placed me among the millionaires of England, and in relating to him in detail Mabel's tragic story of how cruelly she was victimised, I was expressing my mind freely upon the dastardly action of that man who had been engulfed in the subterranean flood, when the kindly monk with the furrowed face raised his hand and, pointing to the great crucifix upon the wall, said in that calm voice of his—"No, no, Signor Greenwood. Hatred and malice should not rankle in the heart of the honest man. Rather let us remember those Divine words: 'Forgive us our trespasses as we forgive them that trespass against us.' As we forgive them! Therefore let us forgive the 'One-Eyed Englishman.'"

The End

A Note About the Author

William Le Queux (1864–1927) was an Anglo-French journalist, novelist, and radio broadcaster. Born in London to a French father and English mother, Le Queux studied art in Paris and embarked on a walking tour of Europe before finding work as a reporter for various French newspapers. Towards the end of the 1880s, he returned to London where he edited *Gossip* and *Piccadilly* before being hired as a reporter for *The Globe* in 1891. After several unhappy years, he left journalism to pursue his creative interests. Le Queux made a name for himself as a leading writer of popular fiction with such espionage thrillers as *The Great War in England in 1897* (1894) and *The Invasion of 1910* (1906). In addition to his writing, Le Queux was a notable pioneer of early aviation and radio communication, interests he maintained while publishing around 150 novels over his decades long career.

A Note from the Publisher

Spanning many genres, from non-fiction essays to literature classics to children's books and lyric poetry, Mint Edition books showcase the master works of our time in a modern new package. The text is freshly typeset, is clean and easy to read, and features a new note about the author in each volume. Many books also include exclusive new introductory material. Every book boasts a striking new cover, which makes it as appropriate for collecting as it is for gift giving. Mint Edition books are only printed when a reader orders them, so natural resources are not wasted. We're proud that our books are never manufactured in excess and exist only in the exact quantity they need to be read and enjoyed.

Discover more of your favorite classics with Bookfinity™.

- Track your reading with custom book lists.
- Get great book recommendations for your personalized Reader Type.
- Add reviews for your favorite books.
- AND MUCH MORE!

Visit **bookfinity.com** and take the fun Reader Type quiz to get started.

Enjoy our classic and modern companion pairings!